Singapore Fling

CARPE DIEM CHRONICLES 2

MAIDA MALBY

EOT Publications

COPYRIGHT

SINGAPORE FLING
Copyright © 2019 by Maida Malby

All rights reserved. Printed by KDP in the United States of America. No portion of this book may be reproduced in any form or by any electronic or mechanical means without permission in writing from the author except for a reviewer, who may quote short excerpts in a review.

This contemporary romance is a work of fiction. Names, characters, places, and incidents either are the products of the author's imagination or are used fictitiously. Any resemblance to actual persons, living or dead, businesses, companies, events, or locales is entirely coincidental.

ISBN: 978-0-9995432-3-8

Edited by Penlight Editing
Cover design by Render Compose

First Edition: October 2019

DEDICATION

*Before you lose your memories of the child
who loved you first, I want to tell you, Mommy, mahal
na mahal kita.*

ACKNOWLEDGMENTS

None of these would be possible without my beloved husband Brian. He's my publisher, my military consultant, and one of my inspirations for Aidan. Thanks, hon. You're my hero. Thanks also to our son Stevie for learning how to cook mac and cheese and roasted duck so he could feed himself while I work.

If not for Linda Hill cracking the whip, I'd still be revising SINGAPORE FLING for the nth time. Thank you, Linda, for helping me place Maddie and Aidan on equal footing.

Lucy Rhodes brought to life Maddie exactly as I envisioned her. That hand-on-hip pose is so ~~me~~ her. Thanks, Luce, for another fabulous cover.

Thanks to my 1201 group, especially Brooke Hoff, Annie Tuiasosopo, and Yulia Lvovna, for serving as consultants, alpha readers, and inspiration.

My first draft was a mess. Thanks to my alpha and beta readers for helping me develop this book into something I am proud to share with the public. Chell Morrow, Gena Gilliam, Preslaysa Williams, Milly Bellegris, Lauriel Masson-Oakden, Susan Schober, Violet Olivo, Ro Merrill, and Tif Marcelo, I owe you all a huge debt of gratitude.

Singapore is one of my most favorite places in the world. I haven't lived there in fourteen years so I'm grateful to Vivienne Wong and Angela Loh for their guidance and corrections. All remaining errors are my own.

Many thanks to OSRBC Writing Group members for reading for me, helping with the cover and blurb, and sharing my social media posts.

Lastly, I appreciate you, dear readers, for supporting my work and for including me and my stories in your continuing love for all kinds of romance.

Again, to everyone, *maraming salamat*.

CHAPTER ONE

Sayang [sa 'yang], n. – In Malay: an endearment; love, dear. In Filipino, an expression of regret over loss of opportunity; "What a pity."

Power. Control. Speed. From the eighth-floor window of her office building in Singapore's central business district, Maddie watched the crimson Porsche convertible cruise along Orchard Road, cutting through the busy traffic on the country's most famous one-way street. She held the strings of the blinds, mid-pull, to admire the sleek German automobile as it rolled to a smooth stop at a red light. Its chrome rims flashed in the January midday sun. With the cloth top down, the car's driver was visible. Based on the glamorous profile, she was either a crazy-rich socialite they called *tai tai* here, or an actress. Lead-footed as well, for the instant the light turned green, the Porsche zoomed out of sight.

Maddie released the strings and clutched the air with her right hand to mime a shift to second gear. Four point four seconds: that was how fast the powerful machine could accelerate from zero to one hundred kilometers per hour.

She pressed her forehead on the glass and sighed with longing. *She* had been that driver not long ago in the Philippines, where she'd owned the same model—a 718 Boxster S, her thirtieth birthday gift to herself last October. It had only been in her possession for seven weeks before she'd been forced to return it to the dealership. They'd bought it back once she told them she'd been transferred to Singapore. It didn't hurt that she had agreed to cover the depreciation cost. Her Porsche was both impractical and unnecessary for getting around this small country with its highly efficient public transportation system.

How I loved that car. She breathed out another wistful sigh. The Porsche was sexy, expensive, hard to get. When she'd driven it, she'd felt admired, envied, and best of all, desired. She'd lost some of that when she returned the car. True, she was in demand for her work, but no one had desired her for a while. Not since …

No. That was over. Only a weekend fling.

It doesn't have to be, a voice in her head whispered. *He lives in the same city as you, and you have his personal cellphone number.*

"That would not be on-brand," she said out loud. For years as a commercial model, she'd cultivated the same image as the Porsche. *Madeleine Duvall is sexy, expensive, and hard to get.*

Madeleine Duvall was also vain, and quite possibly, insane, talking to herself, referring to herself in the third person and rhyming. Who did that? Her, apparently.

Laughter burst from her lips at the absurdity of her thoughts. Mad was a fitting nickname for her, not Maddie.

Still smiling, she reached for the strings again to lower the blinds over the window directly behind her chair, the purpose of standing there in the first place. To give an illusion of heat in the frigid office, she'd raised both sets when she'd arrived at eight, enthused to start a new work week.

Deciding to leave the other set of blinds up, Maddie turned around and started at the sight of her assistant by the open door, left fist raised, about to knock.

"Come in," she invited, still unused to the formality. In the Philippines, her staff had entered straight away and parked themselves on her couch or even on her office table. But this was a different country and a different office culture. She'd give it time—more than the two weeks she'd been here. She'd start with her incredibly efficient administrative assistant, who was exuding an aura of palpable excitement right now.

"*Adik*." Rini addressed her in the Malay form for younger sister as she entered the office. A dusty-pink blush that matched the color of her satin head scarf tinted her brown cheeks. Loose maroon *baju kurung-style* full-length dress swinging around her, the office admin danced in place. "James Bond is here to see you," she said, her voice hushed and awed.

"James Bond?" Maddie echoed. She returned to her desk to double-check who she was supposed to meet at eleven thirty this Monday morning. Exactly as she expected, the paper planner covering her desktop like a giant placemat—Rini preferred the old-school organizer—read "Mr. Ryan" in Rini's neat handwriting.

When she'd seen the appointment on Friday, Maddie had assumed it meant a consultation with Blake Ryan, the CEO of the Philippine branch of a large American manufacturing company, and co-owner of a luxury resort on Boracay Island. Upon taking on a regional role in the Singapore branch of her multinational public communications firm, Maddie had transferred most of her responsibilities from her old office in the Philippines to a local colleague, but she'd kept Blake as a personal client. The company allowed it because they still took their share of the commission.

Blake was engaged to Maddie's best friend, Krista. Wanting to catch up, Maddie had cleared her calendar to have lunch with him after they'd talked business.

But Blake couldn't be the Mr. Ryan outside. She'd had a video chat with Krista last night, and he'd waved from the back. If he was coming, he'd have called out, "See you tomorrow." It hadn't occurred to her then—he'd been on his way out—but it was clear to her now. Blake was Hollywood-handsome and had been likened to the latest Superman, but not to James Bond.

Maddie rubbed her suddenly sweaty palms against her skirt.

That left the other Mr. Ryan of her acquaintance—the Ryan brother she'd tried to forget but couldn't. The lover who'd left her bed without saying goodbye. The man whose call she'd been hoping for since his return from the US with Krista and Blake at the beginning of the month.

Schooling her features into bland interest, she asked, "Which one? Daniel Craig or Pierce Brosnan?

The planner says I'm supposed to have a meeting with a Mr. Ryan."

As her assistant giggled at the mention of the popular actors, Maddie pressed a hand to her stomach in a futile attempt to still the fluttering there. Hunger, not butterflies, she told herself.

"*Betul!* That's correct." Rini confirmed, brimming with good humor. "It *is* a Mr. Ryan. But he looks like a sexy spy. Tall, lean, and dangerous. That's why I said James Bond is outside your office."

Oh! *It* is *him.* Maddie flopped down on her chair, knees too weak to support her. *He's here.*

She flashed an understanding smile at the older woman. Now she got why Rini seemed star-struck with the hunky male waiting outside. She'd been too, when she met him for the first time, last November.

"It's Colonel Ryan, *kakak*," she corrected, adding the respectful Malay term for older sister that Rini had invited her to use. "He's an officer in the US Air Force, not a spy. Please send him in. Thank you. Also, you may take an early lunch if you want." Maddie didn't want to be disturbed in the next half hour, nor to be overheard. She unwound the shawl from her shoulders. The near-freezing chill of the central air conditioning was no match for the heat that had pervaded her body the second her visitor's identity was confirmed.

"*Terima kasih, sayang!*" Rini trilled her thanks and a term of endearment before she left.

How did one greet a most recent former lover? Should she stand or sit? Meet him by the door or wait for him to enter? Maddie lifted herself up, then sat back down again. Standing and waiting by the door would make her look too eager. If she stayed put, the desk between them would give her an air of professionalism. He'd set up an appointment during work hours, after all. Maybe he wanted to hire her company on behalf of the embassy, to manage an event.

That's not what your quivering parts are hoping for. The mocking voice of Mad rang in her head.

Maddie ignored the factual voice and latched on to the unexciting idea. If he was a potential client, the proper way to greet him was with a formal handshake. She should stand.

With her bare toes, she dragged her shoes from under the desk and stepped into them. She'd been sitting with her legs curled beneath her and didn't bother to put on her shoes when she stood to lower the blinds. She stepped around her desk just in time to hear his formal *terima kasih* to Rini. His voice was deep, as rich as the dark chocolate she craved and allowed herself to savor whenever she won a new account. She licked her lips. The thought of the sinful confection she'd associated with Aidan made her somewhat … thirsty.

A moment later, he entered her office, closing the door behind him with a click. Here he was, her weekend lover from two months, nine days, and three hours ago: Lieutenant Colonel Aidan Ryan, Air Attaché at the US Embassy in Singapore. In the flesh. In the tall, handsome, and brooding flesh.

No wonder her assistant had drooled. Aidan did look like Hollywood's idea of a spy, with his close-cropped hair and his all-black ensemble of shirt, pants, and shoes. Maddie wondered if he'd arrived wearing the aviator sunglasses now tucked inside his shirt pocket. For him, they were not a mere affectation. He really was a pilot, and a damned good one if he flew planes as well as he made love. He'd taken her to heights she'd never reached before. He'd—

"Hello, Madeleine."

The sound of her name in his low voice sent the butterflies in her stomach fluttering again. It didn't matter that he'd said it formally. He'd always called her by her given name. One thing she'd learned in their short acquaintance, Lieutenant Colonel Ryan didn't do nicknames.

Fine with her. She could be formal too. Hand extended, she closed the distance separating them in four steps. "Aidan, this is a surprise."

He looked at her outstretched arm with a raised eyebrow over a serious blue-gray eye. Lips with a softness that had astonished her when they'd first kissed were pursed in a thin line. Aloof, as usual, he nevertheless wrapped his large hand around hers with an intimacy akin to a warm embrace. "I scheduled this appointment with your assistant on Friday."

Maddie pulled her hand back in a slow, reluctant retreat. She wanted to keep it there but being close enough to inhale his fresh masculine scent wasn't conducive to keeping her wits sharp. It took her a couple of heartbeats to respond to his statement. "Rini wrote 'Mr. Ryan' on my planner. I thought it was Blake."

"I called from Africa. The connection was poor. She probably didn't hear properly."

Warmth radiated throughout Maddie's body. Aidan hadn't been ignoring her. He'd been out of the country. He'd visited her as soon as he'd come back.

She beamed at him. "Where in Africa? I've been to Johannesburg, Casablanca, and Cairo."

Her smile faltered when Aidan didn't respond to the question. Instead, he said, "You look great, Madeleine."

Maddie flushed. Her beauty was her meal ticket, so she was used to flattery. Aidan's praise pleased her more than she was willing to admit. He hadn't given her many compliments during their weekend fling. "So do you, Aidan."

He shrugged it off, his gaze moving from her face to sweep the room. "Nice office."

She turned to join his visual inspection. It took less than a minute. There wasn't a lot to see: three white walls; a bay of windows across from where they stood, one with the blinds drawn, the other uncovered; her hardwood desk and ergonomic chair in the center of the room, with visitors' chairs clustered in front; and office furniture to the right.

"Thanks." Maddie took pride in making the most of the small space. Framed photos of her on magazine covers hung on the walls. Not entirely because of her vanity. She'd been advised that they instilled confidence among clients about her expertise. Those and the prestigious industry awards displayed prominently on a shelf, along with hardbound reference books. A pot of purple orchids that graced a side table provided a gorgeous burst of local color. Aidan was right. It was nice.

She, however, was not. She'd kept him standing since he'd arrived. "Please take a seat," she said, indicating the red chairs she passed on her way to sit behind the desk.

Aidan flicked them a glance and dismissed them. "No, thank you. I prefer to stand."

He strode to the corner adjacent to the windows. The position placed him in a shadowed area with a view of the entire room, especially the door.

It was a power move, as much as her play to get him to sit in the low visitors' chair had been. Now, he was the one in the superior position.

Although, maybe he didn't think of it that way. He'd done the same in the Philippines every time they'd gone out to eat. He'd always chosen seats with a clear view of the entrance and with his back to the wall. It was probably a military thing. Like his stance right now—standing tall, back straight, chest out, arms at his sides, feet wide apart—at attention, ready for action.

Speaking of the Philippines ... "I heard you're Blake's best man." Maddie crossed her legs and leaned back in her chair. She meant to appear relaxed but tilting her head to look up at him was a literal pain in the neck.

"As I should be," Aidan said with an attitude of the entitlement of an older brother. "And you're Krista's maid of honor."

"As I should be," Maddie parroted in the same haughty tone. She was the bride's best friend, and she'd played a major part in bringing Krista and Blake together in Boracay.

Aidan inclined his head in acknowledgment of their equally important roles. He didn't say anything else, just stared at her with eyes the color of a cloud-filled summer sky—blindingly hot one second, stormy the next.

This was not a business call. If it had been, Aidan would have had stated his purpose by now. The idea that he'd come here to pick up where they'd left off began to take root. The compliments and the smoldering looks sent tingles all over Maddie's body. She had to know for sure.

Her eyes locked on Aidan's, Maddie uncrossed her legs and rose to her full height of six feet when she wore heels, as she did now. With only two inches difference between them, she felt no crick in the neck looking up at him, no discomfort whatsoever. They were on equal footing.

She walked to the window, stopped an arm's length away from him, and pulled the strings to lower the other set of blinds. He didn't blink, not even when the light dimmed with the descent of the window covering.

"I'm also their wedding planner," Maddie said, continuing the thread of their conversation. "Are you here to offer your services?" she purred.

Aidan's mouth lifted at the corners. He braced a shoulder against the wall, appearing more relaxed than he had since he'd arrived. "I'm here to find out what being a best man entails in the Philippines. I'm sure it's more involved than standing beside my brother at the altar to await his bride."

So much for picking up where they'd left off. Maddie raised her chin to hide her disappointment. "You didn't have to come in person if that's all you wanted," she snapped. "An e-mail would have sufficed." She turned to go back to her chair. "I'll give you my business card. Send me a message with all your questions, anytime. There's no rush. We have almost an entire year." She infused her voice with all the professionalism she could muster.

They were idiots, both of them. Him for coming here and giving her hope, her for being disappointed that he didn't want more.

***

Asinine move, Ryan. Madeleine had flirted, and he'd responded by spouting some triviality. He had to do damage control. "I didn't say that's my only reason for coming here to see you," Aidan said to her back, which turned rigid as soon as he spoke.

He pushed off from the wall and approached Madeleine, stopping a foot behind. Enough space for her to feel his presence without crowding her. Enough to touch if she gave him a sign that she'd welcome it. Again.

Aidan was off his game with this woman. He had been from the start. He'd never been indecisive, but where Madeleine was concerned, he struggled with the decision to push her out of his mind or to pull her close. In the end, he hadn't been able to resist the attraction. So he had scheduled an appointment today, his first day back from temporary duty.

"I came here to get to know my future partner in the wedding party better." Aidan stepped forward to whisper, "To tell her I couldn't get her out of my mind. To blame her for distracting me while I was on a mission. To check if she was still available. To—"

Madeleine turned around abruptly, slanted eyes blazing. "You could have led with that, you know."

Whew. "You greeted me with a handshake. All business-like and ingratiating. And …" This ticked him off for a second before he realized it wasn't personal. The room was set up much like his at the embassy, to show who was in charge and it was *not* the visitor. "You asked me to take a seat in a chair so low, I might as well sit on the floor."

Madeleine's green-flecked light brown eyes sparkled with mirth before a seductive glint took over. She placed both of her palms on his chest, smoothing over his shoulders before lacing together at the back of his neck. "Would you have preferred this greeting?" With her lips a hair's breadth away, she whispered, "Hello, Aidan. I'm happy to see you again."

Aidan didn't know who started the kiss. Maybe they did it at the same time. It didn't matter. He'd waited for a sign, and he'd received it.

One hand planted on her plump ass, the other cupping the back of her head, he captured her lower lip between his, opening her mouth to his entry. His tongue swooped in, tangling with hers in hungry thrusts. She met him stroke for stroke, her sweet flavor bursting in his mouth with every pass.

His cock strained against the front of his slacks. Semi-erect since he'd entered her office, now it was at full mast, wanting to match below what his tongue was doing to her mouth up top. To thrust and thrust inside the wet heat until they both came.

Except they couldn't, because an insistent ringing was intruding in their greeting do-over. He withdrew from their lip-lock with a muffled groan. Madeleine moaned in protest, clutching his neck to pull him back. Her eyes remained closed, her face flushed, lips glossy. She tempted him to kiss her again, but he couldn't ignore the noise.

"Madeleine, your phone is ringing." It wasn't his—he'd placed it on vibration mode.

Her lids flew open, her eyes wiped clean of desire. "Shit!" She grabbed her mobile and dropped onto her chair without her usual grace, obviously still rattled by the abrupt ending of their kiss. "Pierre, *je suis désolée,*" she said, apologizing in French to the person on the line.

Aidan caught some of the words like "launch," "media coverage," and "timetable" as he went back to the corner. Her boss? Probably. Blake had taunted him with Madeleine's proximity to the Frenchman when they were in New York over the holidays. Although he hadn't any claim on Madeleine, he'd been jealous and had planned to come here as soon as he returned to Singapore on the fifth day of the new year. But the first thing to greet him when he reported for work was an order to fly to Mauritius.

Mindful of the four-hour difference between the two countries, he'd called Madeleine's office to request a meeting with her. Blake had texted him her mobile number, but he hadn't used it. He wanted to talk to her in person. To verify if his memories of her were real. To find out if she still aroused him with one look. She did. He gazed at her now as she talked animatedly, every now and then typing notes into her computer.

In business attire, her hair pulled away from her face, Madeleine should have looked demure, conservative. But her blouse had a hole beneath a ribbon at the collar that hinted at her tempting cleavage. Her skirt had ridden up, no doubt nudged by his roaming hand, while they kissed. It lovingly encased her shapely hips, but all he wanted was to push it higher, fall on his knees, part her thighs, and feast on the sweet flesh between them.

He licked his lips. Her taste, tart from the lemon-flavored water that sat on her desk, still lingered there. His nose flared at the perfume of her vanilla-scented skin, a scent that pervaded the air in her office as well. What would have smelled too ordinary—too, well, vanilla—on another woman, aroused him on her. It was a perfect mix of sweet but not sugary, warm and slightly spicy, woodsy, and citrusy. *Tart*. Yes, that word again.

They'd begun striking sparks off each other the moment they met in Manila, over two months ago. He'd been cranky and tired that Wednesday morning, having slept only a couple of hours before flying himself to the Philippine capital for a regional security meeting scheduled on the Friday. It was his thirty-sixth birthday, and he'd been raring to get to his brother's Boracay resort for a short break, only to find out he had to wait for another passenger to arrive.

"Hi, guys!" she had sung out to the pilots when she stepped onto the plane, fifteen minutes late. "I'm here. Let's get this show on the road. In the air? You know what I mean." Her voice, smoky and well-modulated, was the kind that usually attracted him. That day, it grated.

Aidan had chosen the seat closest to the rear, to work on a report for the Defense Attaché Office and make efficient use of the waiting time, despite his foul mood. He heard one of the men say, "Nice to see you again, Ms. Maddie." A hint of flirtatiousness in the voice clued Aidan in to the attractiveness of the woman who'd joined him in the small aircraft's cabin.

Presumably, Miss Tardiness was also Miss Beauty Queen. He'd been prepared to dislike her on sight. Habitual lateness was a pet peeve of his; it was a cultural challenge he still needed to overcome in Southeast Asia. Until he'd mastered the adjustment, he'd show her what discipline looked like.

Aidan rose to his feet.

And nearly sat back down.

The woman who approached him was, in a word, breathtaking. Not just any other beauty queen, but Miss Universe-caliber.

Tall and slender, she was both Filipina and Caucasian. Blond-highlighted, honey-colored hair was artfully arranged on top of her head, her sunglasses forming a black crown in the center of the thick mass. Smooth earth-toned skin—miles of it on display, thanks to her skimpy halter top and jean shorts—was luminous, even inside the poorly lit plane. Her eyes sparkled with good humor and a hint of appreciation as she followed his progress to a standing position.

His gaze skimmed her upturned nose but lingered on her red-painted mouth. Her lusciously plush mouth. With the speed of a fighter jet taking off, visions flew through his mind of how appealing those plump lips would look wrapped around his cock.

"Oh, hello," she said, all teeth and charm. "You must be Blake's brother. You look very much like him." She extended her hand. "I'm Madeleine Duvall."

Aidan took her hand in a firm grip and released it right away. He could concede his attraction to her, but he wouldn't let her disrespect of his time go unchecked. "I'm Aidan Ryan, and you, Ms. Duvall, are late. We should have taken off fifteen minutes ago. Please stop flirting with the pilots and take a seat so we can finally depart."

Temper had flashed in her eyes, and her mouth had opened as if to blast him, but she closed it again with a snap. She'd stomped off to a seat at the front, as far away from him as she could get without leaving the plane altogether. Had she apologized, he would have tried to be friendlier. Since she hadn't, he'd kept his distance.

Madeleine's pique had lasted the entire forty-minute flight, and up to their arrival at Blake's hut in the exclusive resort named Perlas. This was the same visual he had then: the back of her head.

But this time, he wasn't cranky, and she hadn't just been chastened. This time, they already had a history. Mainly sexual, but he could work with that.

"*Bonne journée!*" Madeleine ended her conversation with a cheery farewell. She turned her chair around and gasped when she saw him. "Aidan. I'm sorry that took so long. My boss is leaving for Mumbai today and left me in charge of a project," she babbled.

"That's all right. It's only your second offense. You're allowed three," Aidan drawled, knowing it would goad her. A little payback for making him wait again.

"Aidan!" Madeleine pouted. "I wasn't late this time."

"Okay, I'll give you that. You're back at one." She'd apologized prettily; he had to budge. "But, we're going to be late for lunch if we don't leave now." He straightened, ready to go.

Instead of standing, Madeleine leaned back in her chair and crossed her arms in front of her chest. "I must have missed something, because I don't remember being asked to lunch."

Contrary woman. Her assistant had wished him a happy lunch before sending him into Madeleine's office. The older woman had told him she'd reserved a table at the same restaurant he'd planned to take Madeleine. Now, she was retaliating for his counting of her offenses. Fine. He'd play her game.

"Ms. Duvall, may I request the pleasure of your company at lunch today? I took the liberty of reserving us a table for two at Straits." He bowed at the waist in imitation of a gentleman from a classic movie, his smile mocking.

Madeleine's lips twitched at his fake-courtly invitation. "I'm delighted to accept." She reached for her purse as she rose to her feet. "I have to go to the ladies' room first, to fix my hair and re-apply my lipstick. Somebody mussed me up." She tossed this last at him with a saucy grin.

Immense satisfaction surged into Aidan's body. Madeleine's ponytail was askew, and her lipstick was wiped away. He'd done that to her. He could afford to be generous. "Five minutes. You don't need more than that to look beautiful. I'll wait for you in the lobby."

Her eyes narrowed. "Your ability to negate a compliment by issuing an order astounds me." She flounced away, muttering, "Alphahole."

Aidan smiled. Alpha asshole. Sure, he could be one at times. Like now, even if it was just a charade. Good thing Madeleine could handle him. Arrogance was in his nature. Giving orders was his job. He was excellent at it. So was she.

On his descent to the lobby, Aidan identified the emotion coursing through him as anticipation. Before today, his life in Singapore had been safe and placid. Madeleine's arrival promised an excitement he was looking forward to experiencing.

Scratch that. It had already begun.

CHAPTER TWO

Peranakan [per ah nak an], n. – In Malay: a native-born person of mixed local and foreign ancestry.

Maddie bit back a moan at the touch of Aidan's hand on her back as they stepped out of her office building. The sensation of his thumb grazing the indentation of her waist and his fingers squeezing right above the curve of her butt felt like a caress. She suspected he'd done it to arouse her as well as to protect her from the onrush of the lunchtime crowd.

Singaporeans were fanatical about their food; eating was a national pastime. The locals spilled onto the streets at noon on the dot. The numerous restaurants on Orchard Road and the neighboring Scotts Road were packed with people at this time every day.

A sidelong glance revealed that Aidan, like her, had donned his sunglasses. He'd also rolled up his sleeves—*holy sexy forearms, Batman!*—and was intimidating the people coming in the opposite direction. An elderly Singaporean man almost stepped off the sidewalk to avoid the man in black.

How Aidan could look cool in this weather was beyond her. It had taken all of the five-minute deadline he'd given her to fix her hair from a messy ponytail into a tight chignon without the benefit of styling products. Letting it down would have given her a Texas-sized big hair day. Not a good look for her.

Out of consideration for the outdoor weather, she wore a sleeveless cream blouse and an above-the-knee skirt in the darkest lavender, similar to that of a Vanda "Miss Joaquim" orchid, Singapore's national flower. Still, Maddie compared herself more to a wilted blossom than a blooming bud. Only a few minutes in the sun, and she was already sweating, her anti-perspirant having failed to live up to its advertising.

The heat was all over. It rose from the pavement and bounced off the windows of the shops, which were festooned early with next month's Lunar New Year decorations. Red and gold abounded: hot colors, hot everything. The temperature was at the usual thirty degrees Celsius, but the humidity was at an abnormally high ninety percent for this time of the day. The noontime air could only be described as the should-only-be-applicable-to-cake word "moist." Carried by the heavy air, redolent smells wafted to Maddie's nose: a sandalwood scent from an elderly woman, the smoke of incense that clung to the saffron robes of a monk, and *yuck*, the sewage-like stink of ripe durian from the grocery bag of a middle-aged woman.

"Are you okay in those heels?"

Aidan's words made her steps falter. They had turned the corner onto Scotts Road. With less foot traffic, Aidan dropped his hand from her back to his side. He was looking at her purple satin Manolo Blahnik pointed-toe pumps, her favorite pair. The color, texture, and the gathered detail of the Italian-made shoes matched her skirt perfectly, while the pearl beading had almost the exact same shade as her cream top.

"Of course. Why wouldn't I be?" She'd walked runways in shoes with heels taller than these. It was the durian odor and their arrival at the hotel that slowed her, not discomfort from her footwear.

"No reason. I never saw you wear them in the Philippines. You were often barefoot." A gravelly tone entered his voice as he leaned close to whisper, "One day, I'd like to see you wear those heels in bed, your legs around my hips as we fuck. I bet you'll look as hot as you do right now."

He stepped away, leaving Maddie on the sidewalk gaping at him. She fanned her face with her clutch purse. A whimper bubbled up in her throat; she turned it into a breathy thanks for the benefit of the guard who opened the door. She stepped quickly into the five-star American hotel, needing the cool air to relieve her overheated skin. Aidan followed at a more leisurely pace, but he reached the restaurant at the same time she did.

They were met by a smiling *baba*, a Peranakan-Chinese man of indeterminate age with a face unlined and friendly. Maddie recognized him as the manager. There was a moment of confusion when, instead of the table for two in the main dining area she'd had Rini reserve on Friday, he ushered them to a private room at the back. A fully enclosed corner room, it had one wall of windows revealing a balcony outside—the door leading to it was currently closed on account of the daytime heat. After promising to send their server in to take their orders, the manager left.

Maddie flipped her sunglasses to the top of her head and sat on the chair Aidan held out for her, tucking her purse behind her. "Are we expecting more people? These rooms are for groups of at least eight." She had attended lunch meetings in this very same place, even before she worked in Singapore full time. They required a minimum spending of five hundred Singaporean dollars. Not US, but still impossible for only the two of them to spend, even if the hotel lowered the price especially for the US Embassy.

"No. Just us." Aidan sat to her right, a position that accorded him a view of the entrance without being seen himself.

"They allowed you to do that? Isn't that abuse of power, *Colonel* Ryan?" she teased, making a point of stressing the higher rank. He'd once corrected her in Boracay about its use, saying thanks for promoting him, but he was lower in rank—a lieutenant colonel. She later found out, at a weak moment of searching for his name online, that she'd been right all along. Military personnel and civilians addressed officers of both ranks as "Colonel" during conversations.

Aidan removed his shades, showing blue eyes crinkled at the corners. "So, you found me out, huh." He offered a lopsided grin. "You were being haughty, and at the time, you still hadn't apologized for being late. I decided to take you down a notch."

Maddie scoffed at that. "You were being arrogant too. I only tried to match you. And I apologized … eventually." That had stopped their bickering. That, and the feel of his hard muscles beneath her palms as she held on to him when they'd gone jet skiing.

"Eventually. That's the operative word." He smirked.

"*Hmph.* What about the other question?" Aidan hadn't answered her inquiry about which African city he'd been to. She wouldn't let this one go unanswered.

"I requested this particular dining room when I made the reservation. The seating arrangement in the main restaurant is too open for me. I need to have a wall behind my back, and I don't want our conversation to be overheard. This room suited my purposes, and I'm willing to pay for the privilege of privacy and security."

She nodded. He'd been the same in her office: back to the wall, eyes to the door. *This* door was now admitting a server: a short-haired, dark-eyed woman, no taller than five feet. Clad in the traditional *nyonya kebaya*—a figure-hugging embroidered blouse paired with a *batik* sarong skirt—she brought cold towels and a digital device, ready to take their orders.

Maddie was prepared to give hers. "I will have the Hainanese chicken rice and cold bottled water. May I have a glass, a wedge of lemon, and a sprig of mint? No ice, please. Thanks."

The server didn't look surprised by her lunch order. She acted like she'd expected it, like she might have checked it on her pad beforehand.

From the first time she'd tasted this particular meal—one of the country's national dishes—Maddie was addicted. The plain steamed chicken over rice looked simple. But the gingery, garlicky, oily, fragrant goodness of the white chicken meat—even without the skin she had removed from it—and the savory rice boiled in the same broth won her over. She had already eaten the dish five times since she'd arrived in Singapore.

"*Laksa, nasi lemak,* and Coke for me."

Amusement lit up the server's face this time. She repeated their orders, promised to return shortly with their drinks, and left.

Even though Maddie had no intention of ordering anything else, she kept her copy of the menu. She wanted to know what Aidan liked. For future reference.

She found his orders and understood the server's amusement. A spicy noodle soup with fishcake and prawns, and a rice dish with anchovies, egg, peanuts, and *sambal.* At the same time.

Colonel Ryan had a huge appetite for food and for sex. He was her opposite in one way, similar in the other.

Maddie hadn't sampled either dish yet. The *laksa* looked too rich for her, while the *nasi lemak* had too many fried ingredients. If she could find a place where they served low-fat, low-calorie options, she'd try both dishes. But she wouldn't eat them in one sitting, like the greedy man beside her would today.

When she lowered the menu, Aidan startled her by asking, "Since when do you eat rice?"

Maddie reached for the chilled bottle the server had placed on the table in front of her and prepared her drink precisely as she liked it: with freshly squeezed lemon juice and mint leaves clapped between her palms. She took a sip before answering, "Since always."

A lie. Maddie didn't eat rice in the Philippines. Her friends often teased her about revoking her Filipino card. Here, because she couldn't eat the chicken without rice, she'd been indulging since the second day of the year. There was enough Filipino in her that stopped her from eating poultry on New Year's Day. Taken from the chicken's behavior of immediately pecking everything it scratched, the superstition "*Isang kahig, isang tuka*," which could be roughly translated to living a hand-to-mouth existence, countered the wish for prosperity.

Feeling exposed, she lifted her nose at Aidan. "What do you know of my eating habits? We haven't known each other long." A grand total of five days, including their stay in Boracay. "When we were together at my condo in Makati, we …"

"… subsisted on sex and kisses." His voice was deep and husky, his eyes half-lidded, dark blue, no gray at all.

Maddie's cheeks heated. That wasn't entirely true: they'd had food delivered a couple of times. They'd needed the fuel to provide energy for more marathon sex. But that was then, in November. She and Aidan had just returned from a tropical paradise, where they'd witnessed a couple who were close to them get wrapped up in their love for each other. Blake and Krista's romance had rubbed off on them. Mostly the lust, it was too powerful to ignore.

What about now? He'd said in her office that he couldn't get her out of his mind. That he wanted to get to know her better. Were they going to hook up again? For how long?

Bracing her arm on the back of her chair, Maddie turned in her seat to face him. "What are we doing here, Aidan?"

Instead of answering, he held up a finger and stood to shut the door that the server had left ajar. When he returned to the table, Aidan brought his chair next to hers and sat on the edge. With his hard thighs bracketing her legs, he held her complete attention.

His gaze blazed as he said, "We'll be working together to help Krista and Blake plan their wedding, correct?"

"Correct."

"We want each other, yes?"

"Yes," Maddie replied. No need to be coy and deny it. He'd merely stated the obvious.

"Then, we should be together for as long as we're doing this project," he said with an air of someone who would brook no argument on the subject.

Maddie rolled her eyes. *Here we go again with the arrogance.* "Should, Aidan? Like I'm obligated to have an affair with you. Singapore might be small, but you're not the only eligible man here, you know." While she agreed with the idea, she found his presentation a little wanting.

Aidan's eyebrows met in the middle. He scooted backwards in his chair, his posture showing displeasure at her lack of instant acquiescence. "Okay, give me reasons why we shouldn't. Don't tell me you're seeing someone else, because *you* initiated that kiss," he pointed out.

"I did it because I liked what you said at the time. Right now, not so much," she snapped back.

"I'm not good with words, Madeleine. I express myself better with action."

She'd noticed that. Their fling in the Philippines had happened without a lot of words exchanged. He'd shown up at her condo on the Friday night after his meetings at the US Embassy. She'd climbed all over him, and that had been that.

"Fair enough. But, for us to work, we have to meet halfway. I like things laid out step by step. I cannot go from A to B and straight to Z like you do."

"Fine. Let's overanalyze things. Start from the top." Aidan's idea of capitulation left much to be desired.

"All right. A, we don't have to see each other at all to plan a wedding. I can e-mail everything I need from you, and you can respond the same way."

His rejection of that idea came swiftly. "That doesn't work for me. I want to see you."

Aww. "You should have said that."

"I just did," Aidan grumbled.

Maddie delighted in his grouchiness. Who knew he was so much fun to tease? She relented and touched his arm. "I want to see you too, Aidan."

"Then, what's the problem?" The clueless man was sincerely confused. His brows were furrowed, his mouth in a pout.

She held up a fist and stuck out a finger as she counted her reasons. "B, I'm incredibly busy. My clients are from four different continents. C, I travel a lot. D, I often have to work late, sometimes even on weekends."

Aidan's expression cleared. "Missions instead of clients, but you described me almost exactly. That's why when I have downtime, I want to spend it with someone I'm comfortable with. That's you, Madeleine. We've already established our chemistry; I don't want to find somebody else."

Now, *that* made perfect sense. Claiming Aidan as her boyfriend—if that was what he was offering—held many advantages. Primary was satisfying her physical needs. Next was protection from overly familiar bosses and handsy clients. She would have insurance against having to go back to the murky dating pool. Besides, without any friends here, who would go out with her? She needed a diversion, otherwise the days would crawl. She couldn't work twenty-four hours a day, seven days a week. With both of their packed schedules, time spent with Aidan—whether one year or longer—would zoom by as fast as her former car.

She was about to confirm the timeline, but he spoke before she could.

"I get your point, and I'll use my words next time." Aidan glanced at the door before fixing his stare on her. "Fuck it, I'll use them now."

In one smooth motion, he lifted her off her seat and onto his lap. Her legs automatically wrapped around his hips, causing her skirt to roll up to the top of her thighs and expose her flesh-colored silk panties to his heated gaze. The arousal that had hummed between them since their kiss now roared. Blood thrummed in her veins; liquid pooled between her legs.

He pulled her closer until they were chest to chest, groin to groin. With his mouth against her ear, he said in his chocolatey voice, "I'm as hard as I'm sure you're wet. If we weren't in a public place, I'd push aside the silk covering you and eat you out for my appetizer. I might not be the most eligible man in Singapore, Madeleine, but I know I'm the one who can make you come a dozen times a day. At least."

Maddie pressed her face against his shoulder to stop the moan from escaping her closed lips. Not good with words, huh. Damn if she didn't nearly come.

As abruptly as he'd brought her to him, Aidan returned her to her seat and strode to open the door, just in time to hear the squeak of the cart stopping in front of their dining room. She had sufficient time to smooth the skirt over her hips. Outwardly, she projected serenity. Inside, she was a lump of unfulfilled desire.

"*Xiè xiè nǐ.*" Aidan thanked the server in Mandarin after she finished arranging the dishes in front of them. The local woman acknowledged him with a nod and pushed the cart out.

Aidan was right. This room was worth five hundred dollars for the privacy it afforded them to talk and to flirt. The food wasn't bad, either. The smells alone told her their lunch would satisfy. The piquant and savory aromas of ginger, garlic, and soy in her Hainanese chicken rice mixed with the curry and chili of Aidan's *laksa* and *nasi lemak* made for a mouthwatering combination.

Maddie let out the moan she'd been holding in, with the first mouthful of her meal. "Umm."

Aidan chuckled. "Just like that."

Surprised at the unexpected expression of humor, she peeked at him. "What is?"

"The sound you make when you come," he said with a sideways glance, all nonchalance and secret smile. He twisted noodles around the chopsticks with a competence she envied and brought it to his mouth. "Umm," he rumbled deep in his throat, a masculine copy of her orgasmic sound.

Maddie couldn't help her burst of laughter. She shook her head. "You're bad." This reunion was turning out to be fun.

He smirked and continued to eat silently, to her disappointment. She chewed and drank, all the while considering Aidan and his poorly worded proposal for an affair. His arrogance aside, Maddie had no real objections to getting back together. It was what she'd wanted all along. Why stretch out the suspense of her response? She licked her lips and blurted, "Yes."

Aidan took the white napkin from his lap and wiped his mouth with it before tilting his head towards her. "What's that?"

As if he didn't know what she'd meant. "Yes to dating."

"And bedding you?" His eyes gleamed with pleasure.

Smug ass. "Naturally."

"Good." He was back to monosyllables.

"You said as long as we're planning the wedding. Until December?" Maddie asked, to clarify.

She hadn't had a relationship that had lasted *half* a year, let alone one. Colleagues and clients were a no-no, and so were other models. Expats were acceptable. Often European, sometimes Australian, never American.

Never ended today with the man beside her.

Aidan arranged the silverware on his plate. "I never know when and if I'm going to be deployed to a conflict zone or re-assigned after I complete a mission. From experience, that's the longest time I can commit to being based in one place. It helps manage expectations."

Caution: secrets ahead. Message: received. "I see." She had a message to send of her own. "Shall we set some rules?" Her stomach clenched for a second. Would he balk?

A heartfelt groan emerged from him. "As if I don't have to follow enough of those at work," he groused. "What do you have?"

Maddie looked Aidan in the eye as she said, "Honesty, constant communication, exclusivity, and loyalty."

Aidan didn't even blink. His eyes shone with a strange light. "I agree to everything."

It was Maddie who had to look away to emit a relieved breath. That took her less work than she'd expected. She was amazed at how in sync they were.

He finished his drink before saying in a light tone, "When's our next date?"

"*Oof!* That's the question, isn't it?" Maddie took her phone from her bag to consult the calendar. "Hmm. Today is Monday. Tomorrow night is iffy, as I have to prepare for my meeting in Kuala Lumpur on Wednesday. Thurs—"

"I can't on Thursday and Friday," Aidan butted in before she could finish. "How about tonight?"

Maddie nearly gave herself whiplash to goggle at him. "Tonight? We haven't even finished our lunch yet, and you already want to meet again." She was actually quite flattered. Here was more proof that he wanted her. "Do you only go at one speed, Aidan? The speed of light? Sheesh. Let a woman catch her breath first," she admonished teasingly. The man operated at the same pace as her Porsche: one hundred kilometers per hour from go.

"I'm an airman, Madeleine. I don't walk. I fly."

Madeleine rolled her eyes. "Humility is a virtue you clearly do *not* have."

"Facts are facts."

"Yeah, right." Maddie took a last sip of water before rising to her feet. "I'd better get back to work so I can see you again tonight, Colonel I-Fly." She stooped to buss his cheek, pressing a hand on his shoulder to stop him from standing. "Thanks for lunch, Aidan. You don't have to walk me back to the office. I know the way."

He stood anyway.

Maddie danced out of his reach. "Don't kiss me, either. You have curry breath," she joked.

"I was going to give you my card so you can let me know when you're ready, 'Ms. Ginger Breath.'"

He stalked her. She was already by the door when she threw back the words that were sure to irritate him. "No need. I already have your number. Blake gave it to me before he left for New York."

The last thing she heard was his growl. She laughed. Yeah, that was fun, and she didn't even have to go off-brand.

CHAPTER THREE

Flat, n. – In British English: a set of rooms for living in. An apartment.

Bemused, Aidan watched Madeleine as she wandered around his rented apartment, leaving the kitchen to enter the hallway toilet and bathroom. This complex on Napier Road in the Tanglin district was only a mile away from her office building. She hadn't been able to meet him for dinner, so he'd suggested that she come here whenever she finished work. If he had to wait for her, he'd rather do it where he was comfortable. At nine, after he'd given up on her and changed into a t-shirt and cotton sweatpants for sleep, she'd arrived on his doorstep. She'd taken off her shoes, dropped her purse, and declared she was going to snoop around.

It wasn't a big place. The owners' hut in Blake's Boracay resort was probably bigger. Rents in Singapore were expensive. This two-bedroom, two-bathroom, 1100-square-foot flat cost the American taxpayers four thousand Singapore dollars per month. Almost three thousand in US currency when converted. His basic allowance for housing from the Air Force wouldn't have covered it. Aidan was the highest-ranking US military officer assigned to the country at the moment, so he deserved it.

Madeleine came out of the guest room with a frown. Strange that she'd skipped the master bedroom.

Aidan beckoned her to sit beside him on the love seat and handed her a chilled bottle of lemon water he'd bought on his way home from lunch. "Well, what's the verdict?" he asked when she plopped down and tucked her legs beneath her.

She lifted one hand, palm down, and waggled it, the gesture for so-so. "*Comme ci, comme ça.* I like the location. It's close to Orchard, the botanic gardens, and Holland Road. But your unit itself is very basic, just the necessary furniture and appliances. It's impersonal. Nothing here tells me anything about you, except that you're a neat freak."

Aidan didn't have to look around to agree with her. His apartment's spare decor—only what was provided by the State Department—was deliberate. He did not accumulate things. To him, they meant clutter he neither needed nor wanted.

His job often required him to leave at a moment's notice, with only the essentials: his identification and the clothes on his back. Acquiring material possessions held no appeal to him. Everything he owned was replaceable, except his life. Aidan Ryan didn't get attached to anything or anyone outside of his family. Until he'd met the bold and sexy Madeleine Duvall.

Aidan had never entangled himself in a serious affair in any of his previous assignments. Granted, many of those were in hellholes, and the women there were military personnel and local translators. He neither fraternized with his troops nor touched foreign nationals.

Relationships with enlisted personnel, especially those under an officer's chain of command, were watched closely by the military. He didn't need that kind of scrutiny when he was rising up the ranks at a clip faster than most officers.

As for non-American employees at the bases where he served, it was simply a lack of trust. He didn't want to find out the hard way if the woman he was fucking was a spy or a double agent. He preferred celibacy to becoming an instrument of betrayal against his country. Sex often had to wait until he was stateside or on a vacation someplace nobody knew him.

Committing to a relationship with this half-French, half-Filipino spitfire was a first for him. A civilian with no connection to his work, she'd lingered in his thoughts for weeks after their fling had ended. He found her fascinating, in bed and out.

Madeleine didn't kowtow to him. She challenged him instead. She was confident and proud, but not so proud that she couldn't apologize for her mistakes. Before they'd ridden the jet ski together, she'd looked him in the eye and said she was sorry for her tardiness before their flight. She'd given no excuse but promised not to cause him delay ever again. That had earned his respect as much as Blake's endorsement of her work ethic, and her generosity towards Krista.

At his age, Aidan had had enough of meaningless flings. He was ready to try something new with someone different from his usual type. Seeing his younger brother happy and in a committed relationship also had a role in encouraging Aidan to venture into the unknown.

Madeleine poked his arm. "Hey, did I offend you? I was only being honest."

Aidan shook his head, both to dispel his musing and in response to her question. "No. You're right. It's bland. I'm barely here, so it doesn't matter." It was safe and private, the most important requirements for his living quarters. And it was the closest apartment complex to the embassy, a necessity for members of the Defense Attaché Office and the Marine Corps embassy security group. The building's occupants needed to be able to get to the embassy quickly.

"It could use a woman's touch," Madeleine said, her gaze suggestive over the bottled water she raised to her lips.

"Are you volunteering?" Aidan kicked back, resigned to engaging in a long foreplay before he could make his move. Verbal, not his favorite kind. Talking hadn't been in his plans tonight. Madeleine had upended them.

"I can add it to my to-do list when I decorate my own flat," she offered.

"That's generous of you." If that brought her here more often, so much the better. "Where are you staying right now?" He'd asked his brother, but Blake hadn't known.

Her head resting on the back of the couch, Madeleine lifted a languid arm to point in the general direction of the balcony. "At a super-pricey serviced apartment not far from here. Just behind the office."

Made sense. When he'd reported in-country, this place had been prepared for occupancy from day one. Private companies likely didn't have the same system in place. "Have you been apartment hunting?"

"Not yet. Rini got me in touch with a realtor. We'll start looking this Saturday. My first two weeks on the job were spent setting up my life here: work permit, phone, bank account, etcetera. And getting up to speed on my new clients, media introductions. You know, boring busywork." She raised a hand to her open mouth and patted twice, acting out a yawn.

He suppressed a smile at the chagrin on her face when a real one escaped. "If you need help, I might have resources I can share with you. Give me the list of apartments you're looking at, and I'll have them checked against our housing database. For things like security and reliability of the management."

She stretched a foot to nudge his leg. "*You,* high-ranking officer, you, will look it up? You yourself will do it, or will your minions do the research?"

"I will delegate it, yes. Smart ass." Aidan liked this lighthearted banter, but the time for chitchat was over. He scooped her up in his arms and marched into the master bedroom.

"Aidan! What are you doing? Put me down. Right now," she ordered, then followed the words with a laugh.

"You missed one part of the apartment. The most important part. It's time to complete your tour." He threw her onto the king-size bed and jumped in before she could roll out. He covered her body with his, desiring the full contact.

"Get off me, Mr. Caveman. I need to breathe." Madeleine's actions belied her words; she tugged him closer by the shirt before pushing him away with a gentle tap.

Aidan rolled to his side and, raising himself on his left elbow, looked her over. Her perfect grooming was gone. The elastic band she'd used to secure her bun had fallen to the ends of her hair, almost slipping off. Her blouse drooped off one shoulder and was untucked at the waist, and the tongues of the ribbon hung limply down the sides of her breasts. Her skirt had ridden up to show a great expanse of toned brown legs.

He reached out to remove the elastic band and leaned close to nuzzle her unbound hair. The scent of vanilla wafted from her brown tresses. He fingered a lock of hair and brought it close to his nose, sniffing deeply. Odd choice. Too tame for her fiery personality, but it suited her, nonetheless.

She was grinning when he let go of her hair.

"What's the smile for?"

"You. Did you just sniff me?"

"What of it? You shouldn't wear perfume if you don't want anybody to smell you." Or get them aroused, like she'd been doing to him. One sniff got him hard.

"Ha! I don't wear it for anyone but myself. And it should smell good. It was created especially for me in Paris."

He scooted closer. "Let me guess. It's called La Madeleine?" The fingers of his right hand toyed with the hem of her skirt.

"Naturellement. Comment pourrait-il s'appeler autrement?"

The French spoken in her smoky voice seduced him, even when she was acting entitled. "What else, indeed. I like it."

"I really don't need your approval on my personal hygiene items, but thanks anyway."

Aidan frowned at Maddie's mild delivery of the sassy words. He examined her face closely. Her eyelids drooped; her thick eyelashes fanned over her high cheekbones. The yawn she attempted to hide with her hand killed any chance he had of getting relief, except from his own hands.

He flung himself back on the pillow with a harsh, inarticulate sound. "We're not going to have sex tonight, are we?" He was so eager to get into her pants, he'd missed the signs.

With eyes dulled from fatigue, Madeleine stroked his face. "I'm sorry, Aidan. What is it that you Americans say? 'The spirit is willing …'"

"'… but the flesh is weak.'" Great. She'd quoted a bible verse. Way to deflate a hard-on.

"I didn't mean to be a tease."

"You aren't. I should have known when you skipped this room that you only came here to talk." He understood. Madeleine had put in a twelve-hour workday. Naturally, she was tired. That didn't mean he wasn't disappointed. He wished for a second that she hadn't come at all if she was going to leave him sexually frustrated.

He turned over and hopped off the bed.

"Where are you going?" The sound of the bed's movement told him she'd sat up.

Without turning, he said, "I'll change into some running clothes." He meant to work off his frustration even if it rained. "I'll return here on foot after I take you to your temporary lodging." Before that, Aidan needed to take care of his still-engorged cock. He headed for the bathroom.

***

Maddie grimaced as she got off Aidan's heavenly bed to go back to the living room. His bedroom was easily the best part of this apartment. If she stayed there longer, she'd fall asleep. Aidan wanted her gone, and she couldn't blame him. He expected them to have sex. She'd given willing signals at lunch, and she'd said yes to dating and bedding her. He was right. She wanted him. Until she'd found herself flat on her back and exhaustion had caught up with her.

It had been a day. People hated Mondays for a reason. For her, it was the absolute worst day of the week. Today was particularly rough as she'd had to prepare an annual plans presentation for an important client. Pierre's trip to India had doubled her workload. Aidan's visit had saved her Monday from being a disaster, but it had also distracted her so much, she'd spent minutes reliving their kiss and conversation, her reason for being late arriving here. Good thing he hadn't counted it as a second offense. The man was the punctuality police. *Ugh*.

But, he was also thoughtful. Maddie lowered herself onto the couch and reached for the half-empty bottle of lemon water to take a big gulp. It was another *aww* moment when he'd handed it to her. She'd seen the six-pack in the refrigerator along with some cold cuts, cheese, yogurt, and salad. The contents looked almost exactly like hers. She'd bet her Manolos that the bottled water hadn't featured in Aidan's grocery list until today. He had bought them especially for her.

And how did she repay him? By yawning in his face.

Very sexy, Maddie. Not.

"Is there a fly inside the bottle?"

Maddie started at the sound of his amused voice. She turned in her seat to stare while Aidan made his way to her side. He'd changed into a moisture-wicking top and track pants, both black, better suited for walking than the cotton he wore earlier. Again, he looked like the spy Rini had thought he was.

And now, she was wide awake once more. This morning, she'd likened Aidan to dark chocolate.

Wrong.

He was coffee. Black, no sugar, the way she preferred it: strong, hot, addictive.

Maddie let out a sigh filled with regret. She should have jumped him when she'd arrived. In a white t-shirt and gray sweatpants, jaw shadowed by a day's growth of stubble, he had looked totally jumpable. So manly and—

"Madeleine?"

Maddie blinked to bring her focus back to the present. "Hmm?"

"The water. Is something wrong with it? I was sure I got the same brand you were drinking in your office." He sat on the arm of the love seat.

"Oh. No, no. It's perfect. Thanks for getting it for me." A sudden thought popped into her head about something that had been nagging at her. "Why do you keep calling me by my given name?" Everybody called her Maddie, except her mother when she was mad.

"Because that's what you told me to call you." Aidan looked and sounded genuinely puzzled by her question. He moved to sit properly beside her.

"When?" She only introduced herself formally for work.

"On the plane, the first time we met. You held out your hand and said, 'You must be Blake's brother. You look very much like him. I'm Madeleine Duvall.'"

He made it sound like a direct quote. It probably was.

"After which you scolded me for being late." She'd had no excuse then. She *was* customarily late. So she'd closed her mouth and huffed. Nobody ever called her out on her tardiness, except for Aidan.

"Yes, the only other time the issue of names came up was at the restaurant, before we went parasailing."

"You told me to call you Aidan, and I responded by telling you to call me Madeleine." Maddie scooted over to cuddle at his side. He slung his arm over her shoulders. Good. He wasn't mad anymore. Not like then, in Boracay. He was so rude to her, telling her that all she had to do was breathe and men would worship at her feet, except for him. He'd said he wasn't very religious, that the Air Force had beaten it out of him.

Something had changed when Blake arranged for them to share the jet ski and the parachute. They'd had fun together. Aidan's opinion of her had turned positive, especially after she'd belatedly apologized for being late.

I've always had a crush on him.

From the very first moment she'd caught sight of Aidan, Maddie had wanted him. It was lust at first sight. Of course, she didn't let on, but he'd noticed anyway.

"You can call me Maddie." She spoke to his chest, her voice muffled by his shirt. Maybe it was her exhaustion, or perhaps it was his understanding and thoughtfulness, but at that moment, she felt inexplicably shy.

Aidan stroked her hair. "I like Madeleine. It suits you. Sophisticated, beautiful, French."

French. *Merde.* Maddie rose up to see his face. "Do we tell our friends and family about us?" Telling Krista and their squad was a given, but her parents didn't need to know, particularly not her father: her anti-American French father.

Aidan's shoulders moved up and down in a negligent shrug. "You don't need to take out an ad, but you can tell whoever you want. Once Blake knows, everyone who matters to me will find out." The corner of his lips lifted in a slight smile at the mention of his brother.

Blake and Krista. They'd brought her and Aidan together, both in the Philippines and here in Singapore. Maddie would do everything in her power to plan the most fabulous wedding for them. In the process, she and Aidan would see more of each other. They would be dating and bedding one another. She couldn't wait to get started.

"Do you have time to go with me on my apartment hunting this Saturday? We can discuss some ideas for the wedding as well," Maddie suggested.

"Sure. I can do Saturday. What time?"

"The realtor said nine, so maybe a few minutes before that." She hoped she'd remember to set her alarm for eight. Mr. Punctuality here would probably add it to her number of offenses if she was late getting up.

"All right. We'd better get you home, then. It looks like you have a busy week ahead." Aidan stood and held his hand out to help her up.

Maddie accepted the assistance. Before they left, she took one last look at Aidan's empty walls, and thought, *I am going to make this place look so good, Aidan will invite me to stay.*

CHAPTER FOUR

Chope [chawp], v. – In Singlish: to reserve a seat.
Derived from chop; to leave a mark.

"Are you serious about living all the way out here on the East Coast?" Aidan asked Madeleine the moment the realty agent stepped away to give them time to look around the unit on their own. They were on their third apartment of the day. As promised, he had accompanied her as she viewed a couple of units in the west central area of Bukit Timah. Now they were in the southeast, close to the longest beach park in Singapore. Only fifteen miles to travel, but the activity was mind-numbingly tedious. It tested his patience. Being close to noon, he was also getting hungry.

On Tuesday, Madeleine had e-mailed him a list of properties her company had expatriates living in, and he got the embassy's security office to vet them for him. Aidan didn't know her budget, but he figured it was in the same vicinity as his rent. The three apartments they'd looked at this morning were the most recommended. This one—a spacious two-bedroom, two-bath condominium unit that came fully furnished—was priced lower than an apartment in the central business district. Based on her gasp when they'd entered, it was Madeleine's favorite so far.

It was Aidan's as well, for a different reason altogether. He'd had some time to think this past week, and he'd concluded that Madeleine looked right on his bed, in his place. He wanted her there. Often. Perhaps every day. If she rented this condo far away from the central business district, he could offer her the choice to stay at his place during the work week. Even if there were days when she had to work overtime, the opportunities for bedding her would increase significantly, and the need for him to take her on public outings would be minimized.

His challenge now was to get her thinking the same way. He could try reverse psychology. She was smart, this could get tricky.

Madeleine stepped onto the balcony and closed the glass door behind them before answering him. "Why not? What's wrong with the East Coast?" Hand on her hip, Madeleine posed, prepared to defend her choice.

"It's too far from your office." This, the last of the eco-friendly condominiums they'd visited, was twelve miles from the central business district. "It will take you at least thirty minutes to get to Orchard by taxi with normal flow of traffic. In the mornings and evenings, during commute, possibly one hour." He dismissed the bus and MRT train options. Madeleine didn't take mass transportation.

"It's a ten-minute ride to Changi airport. Very convenient for when I leave and come back from business trips," Madeleine stated pugnaciously, her arms now crossed in front of her chest, and her chin set.

There she was. The agreeable Madeleine from Monday night was gone, and in her place stood a woman who knew her own mind. "Can you honestly say you won't be late for work every day?" he challenged, employing his tactic. "No matter how good you are at your job, excessive lateness will be noticed. Singaporeans are sticklers for discipline and order." It was one of the reasons he'd accepted this assignment. He possessed the same qualities.

Madeleine's nostrils flared. Her eyes flashed with fire, the green in them becoming more pronounced as her temper rose. "You are being unfair now, Aidan." She pointed a finger at him. "One time. I was late once, and you've judged me based on it."

Tardiness—a sore topic, check. "Okay. Maybe you won't be late every day. But why would you even want to deal with the bother?"

"Did I say I want to live here? Your line of questioning tells me you think I shouldn't. Maybe I want to now, if only to spite you." Madeleine glared at him.

Aidan barely held back his grin. Nearly there. "Well? Do you like it or not?"

"I do, actually," she confirmed, turning away from him to gaze at the view of the Singapore Strait, the major selling point of this condominium. She didn't see his fist pump.

The gentle breeze from the nearby sea fluttered her sundress against her body. Madeleine already looked at home. Hell, even he appreciated the sight of the white sand, imported though it was, and the water, no matter that it wasn't as blue as many bodies of water in the region. The taste of salt in the air, the scent of brine, and the sound of waves lapping against the shore all explained the appeal this place held for Madeleine.

"But there are other considerations." She turned back to him with brows drawn.

Shit. He'd congratulated himself too soon. "Like what? Like this condo is on the thirteenth floor?" He didn't believe in the superstitions. Maybe Madeleine did. He hoped not.

"It is not. It says 1201," she said with a laugh.

"Yeah, but in Singapore, like in the UK, there's a ground floor then a first floor," he replied.

"Huh. I never paid attention."

"Now you know."

"What else?" Her lips turned up at the corners.

She was messing with him. Did she catch on to his scheme? He changed tacks. "You should never live on the fourth floor."

"Because the Chinese and Japanese pronunciation of four sounds like death. That doesn't apply here, but yes, I know."

"I was referring to the apartment near Dairy Farm," he said. That condo was a mere seven miles away from Orchard. Not far enough for his idea to work. She had to choose this place.

"Which one?"

"I don't care. Those are nightmare locations, too." The other two apartments they'd visited were close to the nature park.

"Why? Because of the forest?"

"Yes. And again, too far." The lie tripped easily from his mouth.

"How can anywhere be too far in Singapore? It's a small island. Only fifty kilometers from east to west, twenty-seven from north to south. You can go around it in one day."

"Anywhere I can't walk is too far."

"Aidan Ryan, you are being ornery."

"I'm a grumpy bastard. I thought you already knew that about me."

Madeleine laughed and hooked her arm around his. "What you are is *hangry*. We should go and grab some lunch. We'll resume our hunt later."

Hell, no. "That's the best suggestion I've heard all morning." He meant the lunch.

"I'll tell the realtor I'll call him when we're ready to see other condos."

Not if I can help it. "You do that."

***

Maddie looked askance at all the food Aidan had ordered from various stalls at the East Coast Lagoon Food Village, the closest hawker center to the last apartment. All the major Singaporean ethnic groups were represented: Chinese, Malay, and Indian. *Char kway teow*, a fried noodle dish with several types of noodles in brown sauce, with strips of fishcake and some *kailan* leaves; several sticks of mixed meat *satay*—pork, chicken, and mutton—which was the one meal she'd asked him to get for her; and *murtabak*, flat bread tossed in the air like pizza, rapidly cooked in oil, filled with mutton, chicken, onion, and peas, and served with curry.

She had sat at a table hidden by palm trees— the farthest one from the hawkers and other diners because Aidan was paranoid—while he'd gone and ordered the dishes. Neither of them had a pack of tissues or an umbrella to leave on the tabletop to "*chope*" it, as the locals did. Aidan paid as the food was delivered, giving each vendor a tip nearly equal to the price of the food. He scowled at her when she paid for the satay and muttered under his breath at her reciprocal glare.

"I can't eat all these," Maddie protested. The smells alone filled her up. She swore she'd gained five kilos easily, from inhaling the smokiness of the meats and pungency of the sauces.

"I can. Eat what you want, and I'll finish the rest." Aidan was already halfway through his plate of noodles.

Maddie took one stick each of every kind of meat, a few spoonsful of cucumber salad, and one small square of *murtabak*, which she wrapped first in napkins to wipe off most of the oil. She didn't add the *satay*'s peanut sauce to her plate. It was too thick. The marinade on the meat was enough flavor for her. Thankfully, *satays* were fire-grilled, or else she wouldn't eat them at all.

Aidan had no such hesitation. He ate everything, including the *pandan* sticky rice that was part of the *satay* dish. She'd been right when she'd said he was *hangry* earlier.

Full from the serving she'd finished, Maddie patted her lips with the paper napkin. "How can you eat like this and stay so lean?" She'd had to spend two hours in the gym every night this week to make sure the chicken rice didn't stick to her thighs.

"I walk everywhere. And I only eat like this at lunch, never for dinner."

"What about breakfast?" They'd slept in on both Saturday and Sunday mornings in Makati. She never found out what he ate at the start of the day.

Her question made him look up from his meal. One side of his mouth tilted sexily. "You can find out for yourself. Spend the night at my place."

Smoldering ensued, but she resisted. "I suppose." It wasn't quite the invitation she'd been angling to get. She wanted more than one night.

"You blow me away with your enthusiasm," Aidan drawled.

Maddie had to laugh. "I want to, but I can't tonight. I have a dinner with the agent of a prospective client. And it doesn't make sense to sleep over somewhere a mile away while I live in an apartment just behind my office building."

"When do you have to move?"

"Anytime I've secured my own place. The company offered me a perk. I'll receive whatever amount I don't use for the serviced apartment, so I have funds for deposit and advance." She hadn't rushed her flat search because she wasn't worried about funding the necessary requirements using her own cash. Still, free money was welcomed, especially since here in Singapore, the company paid salaries once a month instead of the bimonthly frequency in the Philippines. She wouldn't receive her first paycheck until the end of the month. Ten more days of dipping into her accounts.

"You should have told me sooner."

"Why is that?" Maddie asked with false innocence.

"You could have stayed with me this past week and kept a couple of thousand dollars more for yourself."

Aaah, how she loved hindsight. "The topic didn't come up in our conversation, and it's not something I can casually drop. We only reconnected on Monday. I couldn't be presumptuous." She wasn't *that* forward. Also, Aidan had to issue the invitation. She wouldn't go where she wasn't wanted.

Aidan moved closer to her on the concrete bench. "Would you like to stay with me while you finalize your apartment search?" he said in a low voice.

Bait taken. *Ladies and gentlemen, meet Madeleine Duvall, fisherwoman.* "If it's not an inconvenience, I'd appreciate that. Thank you," she said, demurely.

He looked deep into her eyes. "You do know I have an ulterior motive for having you there, right?"

Bedding her. "You have a one-track mind," Maddie admonished, even as she heated at the thought of going to bed with him again soon.

"Just a normal red-blooded male."

The statement rubbed her the wrong way somehow. "What is normal for you, exactly? Do you require sex daily? Once a week? Twice?" It had been eleven weeks since they last had sex. Did that mean there'd been someone else? If so, how many?

Aidan raised her chin with a finger, pinning her with his blazing blues. "This is not the place for this conversation, Madeleine. But, if you're asking if I've fucked anyone since I left your bed in November, the answer is no." He leaned forward until his warm breath tickled the fine hairs around her ear. "If you're asking how often we'll have sex once you're in my bed, the answer is ..." He paused for effect, causing her stomach to do a backflip. "... until you beg me to stop."

Maddie let out a shaky breath. With as much bravado as she could muster, she said, "I don't beg, Aidan."

He flashed her another one of his lopsided grins. "In that case, we'll both die happily from exhaustion." Acting satisfied that he'd had the final word, Aidan shifted back to the center of the bench and gathered their used paper plates and plastic cutlery, then he stood to throw them in the bin.

Cocky ass. Heart light from relief, Maddie followed. There was no use staying at their table. They had more to talk about, and as he said, this wasn't the proper place for it.

"Have you made a decision? Are we done with apartment hunting?" Aidan asked when she joined him to walk towards the taxi stand.

She had—the seaside condo—but she didn't want Aidan to withdraw his offer for her to stay at his place, so she fibbed a little. "Not yet. I want to see a couple more before I choose. Shop around. There might be ones along River Valley that won't cost half of my monthly income." Though her compensation was high, it didn't make sense to spend a lot of it on rent. She spent her money on things she could own. An apartment in Singapore wasn't one of them.

The Philippine government was chaotic at times, but it was her birthplace and where her best friends lived. It was still home. At the end of her three-year contract, she planned to go back, unless a better-paying opportunity came along elsewhere. For now, she'd enjoy Singapore and all it had to offer. Including this red-blooded alpha male who was scowling again.

"Is it imperative that we do them today? There's no rush now, is there?"

Such a guy. Mention shopping and he balked. "No. We don't have to see more today. If I don't have a business trip, I'll go again next weekend."

The curve of his mouth reversed from down to up. "Excellent. Let's move you in to my place then, shall we?"

Threading her arm through his, Maddie said, "We shall."

CHAPTER FIVE

Atas [at us], adj. – In Malay: a person or place that is high class.

"Thirty-one pairs of shoes. Remarkable," Aidan murmured, his gaze following Madeleine while she stacked shoebox after shoebox against the wall in the smaller bedroom. Add those to the mountain of clothes and accessories in the tall pile of suitcases on the floor, and she could start a boutique in his apartment. They'd required assistance to take everything from her room down to the lobby in her serviced apartment and needed three trips to bring them up here to his unit. He'd anticipated a short trip—it turned into a three-hour production that lasted until four in the afternoon. Even with his help, Madeleine had taken an hour to pack, since they'd had to find proper containers to transport her precious Italian and French footwear collection.

Aidan had come into the room to tell her he'd cleared some space in his walk-in closet and master bath, but he got distracted by her and her things. No wonder she wrinkled her nose at his lack of stuff. She had loads of it.

According to Madeleine, these shoes were only what she'd brought from the Philippines and what she'd purchased during the three weeks she'd been here. She'd left a few pairs behind in her condo. How many were a few? A hundred? Or, maybe over a thousand like her country's former First Lady. "Is this a Filipina thing?" he asked when she finally straightened from her task and looked up to see him standing by the open door.

Madeleine walked up to him, stopping when they were toe to toe. Well, toe to shoes. Funnily enough, she was barefoot—an actual Filipino thing. Hip cocked and perfectly drawn eyebrow raised, she poked him in the chest with a manicured finger. "Are you seriously calling me stereotypical, Aidan?"

This was her tell, her invitation to flirt: getting close but still keeping a short distance away. For all Madeleine's sophistication and communication skills, she didn't express her desires out loud. She'd make the first move, signaling consent, then wait for him to interpret her cues. This time, Aidan didn't misread them. He grinned down at her and quipped, "If the shoe fits." In truth, she was the exact opposite. Neither Filipina, nor French, Madeleine was uniquely her own person.

She poked him again, eyes glinting with appreciation. "Ha ha. You know it doesn't. Too narrow for me," she said. "Your mom and sister don't own a lot of shoes?"

Aidan made a grab for her hand—he preferred her sharp claws to score his skin, to scratch him, to dig into his back in the throes of passion, not during a casual conversation—but she pulled it back quickly and side-stepped him to place herself out of arm's reach.

"No," he said, pivoting to head to the master bedroom across the narrow hall. They were not going to do the same dance they had on Monday night.

As he anticipated, Madeleine followed. "They don't? That's unusual. What about your former girlfriends?"

Aidan stopped at the foot of his king-size bed and turned to face her. "No," he said again, placing his hands on her waist and pulling her flush against his hardening body. Almost as a reflex, her arms looped around his neck, her beautiful face watchful.

"I don't want to talk about shoes." His hands skimmed along her sides, one stopping at the underside of her breasts, the other threading through her waterfall of hair. "I don't want to talk at all." With a gentle tug, he tilted her face at the same time he lowered his mouth to capture hers.

She responded the way he'd hoped: quickly, and with equal fervor. Her mouth opened to let him in. Their tongues thrust and parried against each other, well matched, both giving and taking. Beneath his own mint flavor, he tasted her lemon and vanilla. Tart and sweet. With her crusty exterior and soft interior, Madeleine reminded him of another thing he liked that bore the same name: the baked variety. Like madeleine pastry, she was utterly delicious. He couldn't stop at one bite, he wanted more.

Aidan deepened the kiss, with desire's grip on him tight and complete. His right hand roamed over her back, down her ass. He gripped, clutched, squeezed. Smooth skin, supple flesh, fragrant scent, she was seduction personified.

The sound of her withdrawal came first—a moan at the back of her throat. She broke the kiss and took a step back. He reached for her, but she held out a hand to stop him. A growl stayed in his chest when she lifted her hands to her shoulders and tugged at the spaghetti straps of her sundress. Already turned on from their kiss, her slow reveal of golden skin ensured his readiness. He wanted to pounce but had to wait. She still wore her strapless bra and boy short panties. Nude silk. Ultra-feminine. Sexy as hell.

To his frustration, Madeleine didn't remove them. She lifted her chin in challenge. "Your turn."

Barefoot and wearing barely-there lingerie, she should have looked ridiculous issuing orders. Instead, she looked fierce, magnificent. She would look even better if... "I will. Do something for me first. Go back to the other room and grab a pair of heels." The visual of those stilettos digging into his ass while he plunged into her excited him. First, her claws. Now, her heels. *Since when did I become a masochist?*

It seemed to have the same effect on Madeleine. Her eyes turned molten, and her skin took on a becoming blush. Hair flying, she took off for the other room.

With equal haste, Aidan grabbed his shirt by the collar, pulled it over his head, and tossed it to the floor to join Madeleine's dress. Next, he tackled his belt as he simultaneously kicked off his shoes, uncaring where they landed. He was about to reach for his zipper when two gorgeous legs filled his vision.

Two strips of leather—dark gray, almost black, the same shade as the F-15 Eagle fighter jet he flew in Afghanistan—fastened her shoes. Half a foot of dagger-like metal raised her ankles skyward. No wonder stilettos were named after a weapon. They looked lethal. So did the woman wearing them.

"Need help?"

Aidan reluctantly lifted his gaze from her feet to her face. She stared at the hard-on tenting his slacks. "Have at it," he invited, thrusting his hips forward.

In two strides, Madeleine's hands were on his zipper. Aidan held his breath in anticipation. It came out in a hiss at the first contact of her skin on his body. This was torture, plain and simple. She enjoyed tormenting him. Her tongue was caught between her teeth, lips wide with glee at holding him in the palm of her hand. Literally. She cupped him as she lowered the zipper agonizingly slowly, seemingly one tooth at a time.

"Hurry up, Madeleine," he gritted out, voice roughened by desire.

"Patience, Colonel I-Fly. I don't want to hurt your … um … precious package," she said, not even hiding her laughter. "You should have taken your phone out of your pocket first. It's tight in here."

"I'll get back at you for this." He clenched his fists to stop himself from flinging away her hands and finishing the job himself.

"Promises, promises." She pulled harder on the zipper until she reached the end. "There. All done." With one final squeeze, she released his cock. His pants dropped to the floor with a thud, his phone, wallet, and keys aiding gravity in their quick descent. They both jumped as a trill pinged from the discarded clothing.

"Damn it, not now!" Aidan barked.

"*Aargh*," Madeleine screamed in frustration. She flopped down on the bed and removed her heels. Frowning at him, she said, "You'd better answer it, Aidan. We both know nobody calls on Saturday afternoon without a good reason."

"You have got to be kidding me." Crouching, he fished the offending piece of shit technology that had intruded on his personal time out of his pants' pocket. A snarl escaped his lips when he saw the name on the caller ID. He reined his temper in before pressing the answer button. "Ryan here, how may I help you, Ambassador?"

With the phone tucked between his ear and shoulder, Aidan got to his feet and restored his clothing while he listened to the presidential appointee explain why he'd called.

An American citizen had been arrested for violating Singapore's strict drug laws. The man claimed to be an Army veteran, and the drugs in his possession were supposed to treat his post-traumatic stress disorder. Even though the State Department had protocols in place for such a situation, this ambassador, a top presidential campaign contributor, needed his input before deciding how to respond to the request for assistance. Singapore dealt harshly with drug offenders, particularly those with the intent to traffic them. Punishment was mandatory execution: by hanging. That, of course, needed to be prevented—the ambassador didn't want it on his conscience if he could have stopped it from happening.

There was nothing he could do but say, "Yes, sir. I'll be there in fifteen minutes." Poor timing notwithstanding, he welcomed the task and the opportunity to curry favor with the chief of mission, who was totally unqualified, but still his immediate superior in his assignment here in Singapore. Unfortunately, Aidan had to leave an unsatisfied woman in his bed in exchange.

The woman who was now sweeping past him to return to the guest room. She'd gotten dressed as well.

"Madeleine," Aidan called out to halt her progress. He hated feeling like he needed to apologize for something that wasn't his fault.

She turned around with a soft exhale. "I get it, Aidan. You have work. It's the reason we're both here in Singapore. I'll be fine."

Relieved, Aidan stepped close and took her hand in his. "I know you will." It was the truth. "What I don't know is how long I'll be gone. I left a set of keys for you on the coffee table and added your name to the list of authorized occupants for this unit. You can come and go as you please and use the pool and gym anytime you want." He'd been busy while she'd packed. The temporary authorization was good until the end of February. He planned to extend that on Monday. It was one of the favors he meant to extract from the ambassador.

"Thank you." Madeleine laced her hand with his and squeezed. "I'll unpack what I'll need this week before I go to my business dinner tonight. Hopefully, we'll both be home by nine … -ish?" Her tone held promise.

"Hopefully." He raised their joined hands and pressed his lips to the back of her wrist before slowly letting go. Her sharp inhale assured him that he could inflame her with one touch, and vice-versa. "Be good, Madeleine."

"I'm always good," she shot back.

Not always. Sometimes she was naughty. Like earlier when she fondled his dick. He liked Naughty Madeleine. A lot.

***

"Guys, where are you?" Maddie asked the blank screen of her tablet. Had *M'amie* not received her text to join her for a group chat? No one from her squad had responded yet, not even Krista. It wasn't that late—just nine thirty pm. They hadn't chatted as a group since her farewell dinner with everyone but Krista before she'd left for Singapore at the end of the year. She missed her *barkada*. Didn't they miss her too? *Ten more minutes*, she thought, settling herself comfortably in what was becoming her favorite spot on the love seat in Aidan's apartment. Then, she'd give up and get ready for bed.

Tonight had been a bust. She'd made her excuses early at dinner and rushed back here at quarter to nine. He'd called at nine o'clock on the dot to tell her another matter needed attention, requiring him to stay longer at the ambassador's residence. That had sparked the urge to speak to her long-time friends.

Who slept before ten anyway? Not Maddie. Especially not on a Saturday night. If she was in

Manila, she would have gone out again. She would have been partying, dancing, being photographed for the Sunday newspaper's society pages. None of that was likely to happen here in Singapore because she had only a handful of local clients. So, here she was, staying in by her lonesome. It was the exact situation she hadn't wanted to find herself in, hence her acceptance of Aidan's offer to be together.

It wasn't that she needed a man in order to be happy. Boyfriend-less Maddie had been content in the Philippines. Someone from *M'amie* was always there to call on for a chat, even after two of them got married and had babies, especially Krista, who didn't use to date. Now that Krista had acquired a fiancé, her priorities had changed. Blake had become number one. Maddie, so far away in Singapore, had been relegated to sixth place behind the four Lopezes: *Tito* Arsenio, *Tita* Marissa, Alex, and Farrah. Maybe even seventh since Krista had discovered her dad in the US.

Maddie swallowed past the thickness in her throat and fought the onset of tears. Apart from herself, nobody considered Maddie their number one priority; not Krista, not her parents, not Aidan. She needed to remember that. This affair was temporary, a mere one-year fling. Her and Aidan's relationship was only physical. They were together for companionship and convenience, nothing more.

Don't forget that, Madeleine. Do not get attached to Aidan. Keep things light. No angst, no tears. This is just a Singapore fling. Okay?

No, it wasn't okay. She heaved a sigh. So, this was how it felt to wait. Was it karma? Payback for all the times she'd been late? "This sucks. *M'amie* sucks. I'm going to—"

Her tablet lit up with an incoming video call from the group. Before clicking on the accept button, Maddie blinked several times and straightened her spine, making sure her friends would not be able to detect any sign of vulnerability in her carefully built facade.

"Finally!" she said, throwing her arms in the air for effect the second Krista's and Angela's images appeared. Arrogance was expected of her. Sad face, never.

"Apologies, Your Grace. I couldn't stop in the middle of EDSA to answer your imperious summons," Angela replied with an eye roll of her own, citing Manila's major thoroughfare Epifanio Delos Santos Avenue.

Despite herself, Maddie smiled at the pushback. A head shorter than her and Krista, Angela packed an outsize personality in her petite frame.

Maddie turned her attention to Krista, who was smiling gently. "And you, Krissy? Too busy canoodling with Blake?"

"*Uuuuy! Baka nga.*" Angela piled on the teasing. She agreed with Maddie's supposition about Krista's late response.

Krista laughed. "No. We just returned from watching a movie. Canoodling comes later."

Her best friend had come a long way from the blushing virgin to the confident woman of today. "Where are Lisa and Jenny?" Maddie asked.

"Probably sleeping already. They both have young kids, you know," Angela replied.

Add selfish to her character flaws. She hadn't thought of that. "Oh well. I'll try to catch them during the daytime."

"What's up? Do you speak with *lah, leh,* or *mah* yet? Are you coming back for Chinese New Year? Have you found a flat already?" Angela threw the rapid-fire questions at her. "I have to go there in June to renew my passport. Can I stay with you?"

Maddie answered the last couple of questions first. "Not yet. I only started apartment hunting today. I'll probably get a two-bedroom unit, so of course you can stay with me when you come for a visit. You too, Krista."

Angela gave her two thumbs up while dancing on her seat, dimples flashing. The woman didn't know how to stay still.

"That'll be nice. Are you sure you don't need three bedrooms? The second for guests and another for your extensive wardrobe?" It was Krista's turn to tease.

"Says Imelda Jr. herself," Maddie shot back. While she had more bags, Krista's shoe collection exceeded hers in terms of quantity, if not value.

"As if anybody who's ever met both of us will believe that. Don't forget, I'm living in your place, where one bedroom resembles the high-end section of SM," Krista scoffed.

"All right already. *I'm* the one with the most shoes. *Sheesh*!" Angela butted in. "If the two of you are done arguing over who is more Imeldific, I'd like to go to bed now *na*. I have to fly to Palawan tomorrow. La Reine Madeleine, please tell your loyal servants your big news."

Maddie opened her mouth to deny Angela's assumption but closed it again with a snap. It was no use. They knew her too well. She took a deep breath, and said, "I'm in a new relationship." She didn't know how to label Aidan. Lover? Boyfriend?

She took a peek at Krista's expression: huge smile, knowing look. Unsurprised.

"*Carpe diem*, seize the day *ang peg*," Angela exclaimed. "You've only been there for three weeks. Fast, *ha*. But then, it has been two years since you had a guy. Who with? Is it your boss?"

"No," both she and Krista blurted.

"Huh? How come Kris knows already?" Angela's lower lip jutted out in a pout.

"Because it's Blake's brother Aidan," Maddie explained. She hadn't told Krista about the weekend fling after Boracay. There hadn't been any need. Krista and Blake had already guessed. Blake had given her Aidan's number and had most likely given hers to his brother. They'd played matchmakers.

"Wow-wow-wee! Is he as handsome as Blake? How did you two meet? Was it on a plane like your most recent ex-boyfriend, that French architect, Jeremy? Does Aidan work there too? How come I haven't heard anything about this guy?" More *rat-tat-tat* questions from Angela.

Because there was nothing to tell before. "Aidan is better-looking than Blake. Yes, we were on the same flight to Boracay when I went there for Krista's birthday," Maddie started.

"Blake is more handsome, and it was also Aidan's birthday," Krista asserted.

There was no proof that Aidan had been with them. He hadn't allowed himself to be photographed, so the pictures their friends had seen only had Krista, Blake, and herself in them.

"So, you met on November two. Not so fast, *pala*. Bet it was insta-lust. Aaaand?" Angela shifted her gaze between the two of them.

"And he came to the office on Monday. We had lunch, then he accompanied me apartment hunting this morning," Maddie finished, leaving gaps as large as the Flower Dome at Gardens by the Bay.

"Fine. Don't tell me the juicy parts. I'll fill in the blanks myself. I have such a vivid imagination, I could be a writer. How is he? Is he nice?" Angela leaned closer to the screen, eager to hear more.

"He can be an alphahole."

"Yes, he's nice."

She and Krista spoke at the same time. The insult came from her, the affirmation from Krista.

"So, this guy is nice to Krista, but he clashes with you. That's why you're with him." Angela snapped her fingers. "I get it. *Bagay kayo*," Angela concluded, saying Maddie and Aidan suited each other perfectly.

"I agree," Krista said with an emphatic nod. "You two are a good fit. He can't dictate to you as you won't allow it, and you don't intimidate him since he's successful himself. You don't really think he's an alphahole, do you?"

"No," Maddie admitted begrudgingly. "I wouldn't call him nice, though."

"Well, neither are you. Look at that. You've met your match," Angela declared. She cackled like the witch she sounded like at the moment.

Maddie wasn't offended, but she couldn't let Angela get away with the taunt. She tapped a finger on her chin. "I'm not nice, huh. Guess you don't really want to stay at my place. *Sayang*. The one I like the best and will probably choose is close to Changi and to East Coast Park, *pa naman*. Didn't you tell me that's where you want to live if you ever move back to Singapore?" She shook her head and let out a mournful sigh. "*Quel dommage.* Too bad, so sad."

Angela pointed a finger at her. "You, Madeleine Duvall, are *not* nice." She clasped her hands in front of her chest. "But, you are the most generous, incredibly talented, utterly sophisticated, impossibly gorgeous—"

"*Sipsip!*" the usually proper Krista heckled, making slurping noises at Angela's fawning superlatives.

Maddie's lips twitched. Glee bubbled up inside her until it couldn't be contained, and she had to laugh. She needed her best friends tonight, and they'd come through for her. They supported her and made her happy. "Fine. You're back in my good graces," she said to Angela.

"*Yehey!*" Angela cheered. "And on that note, I'll say good night. I really have to sign off. I'm leading a dive tomorrow, and I need my beauty rest. Great to catch up with you, Mads. See you soon, Kris." With a wave, she clicked off.

"Okay, tell me the rest of it," Krista urged.

If anybody had Maddie's number, it was Krista. "I'm staying at Aidan's place," she confessed.

Krista's eyebrows rose so high, one of them disappeared behind her side part. "Oh, really? What happened to Miss Independence?"

"It's only temporary. I'll still get my own condo, like I said earlier. We're both so busy, we barely saw each other this past week, despite agreeing on Monday to date," Maddie explained, hoping she sounded matter-of-fact rather than defensive. "In fact, he's not here right now. He got called in to the embassy."

Krista nodded. "I completely understand that. Blake and I work for the same company, and yet we don't see each other every day at the office. We live in the same building, thanks to you, but sometimes we don't meet at all. You and Aidan need to create opportunities to be together so that you'll get to know each other better."

Hmm. Her best friend was giving her total support, with neither admonishments nor warnings. When it had been reversed, before Krista had decided on Blake, Maddie warned her to be careful with her heart. None of that was forthcoming. Huh. "That's it? No 'make sure you don't fall in love with him' warning?"

"Ha ha ha. No. I like Aidan for you and you for him. You will soften his hard edges, and he will take care of you, even if you don't think you need him to. I'm one hundred percent for Team Aiddie or Maidan. I think you'll be good for each other. I really do."

Wow. Maddie felt her heart swell with affection for her best friend, the sister of her heart. She wasn't number one in Krista's life, but she was still important. Still loved.

"I love you, Krissy." Maddie only ever said that to two people: her Ma and her best friend. She'd never said it to either of her parents. If her papa said it to her, she'd probably say it back, but it hadn't happened yet.

"I love you too, Mads. And I miss you so much." Krista brushed away tears from her eyes. "But if you were here, these wonderful things wouldn't happen in your life, so I've accepted that. Let's do this often. Check in regularly, *okey*?

"Definitely. We have your wedding to plan, after all. Boracay at Christmastime, right?"

"*Korek*. Just a small one. The three families: the Ryans, Lopezes, and O'Connors, plus *M'amie*, Blake's partners at the resort, and a couple of people from work."

The O'Connors were the family of Krista's biological father. That reminded Maddie of the other thing she'd wanted to discuss with Krista. "Kris, I met a prospective client today. A guy who's representing the so-called Bad Boy of American Golf."

"Oh." Krista's brows knitted. "Patrick?"

"Your half-brother's management company thinks he should celebrate his Filipino roots to win over global fans, increase his endorsements, and sell more products for his sponsors. And they seem to believe I'm the best person to handle his image rehabilitation from this side of the world, because of our similar backgrounds."

Maddie was happy that Krista had gained a new family. Another father, a new aunt, and two half-brothers. But, she was also indignant that this particular half-brother was giving her best friend grief over the discovery of their shared DNA. "I'll recommend another consultant if you don't want me to take him on."

Shaking her head, Krista said, "Mads, you are the best at what you do. Don't turn him down just because he hasn't fully accepted me yet. He can learn a lot from you as far as making the best of both Filipino and foreign heritage. It will not only be good for his career but will also make his mother happy."

Maddie had had no choice but to embrace her dual heritage. She wasn't Filipino enough. Nor was she French enough. But, combined, she was *more*. It had been her unique selling point. To deny it meant she became a nobody. "All right. But I'll make it clear to him that the moment he disparages you within my hearing, I'll drop him on his ass so quickly, he won't know what hit him."

Krista laughed. "I'm sure he'll behave. You're scarier than me. When will you meet him?"

"Tomorrow. He's playing at the Singapore Open. Doing well, actually. He's leading the tournament." Despite his on-course tantrums, Patrick O'Connor was an exceptional golfer. Having him as a client would be beneficial to her portfolio. If she did well with him, Maddie was certain she could get more sports personalities and international celebrities as clients.

"You have to work on a Sunday? *Aray*. You really have no time to go out on dates," Krista said with a wince. "Why don't you invite Aidan to go with you so you can spend some time together? My dad is Aidan's godfather," Krista informed her. "I'm sure he'd want to see Patrick."

"Yes, I was already thinking of doing that. Patrick's rep gave me two tickets."

"All right then. Give Aidan a hug and say hi to Patrick from me."

A touch of sadness pinched Maddie's chest. Krista was about to call it a night. "Oh, canoodling time?" she said in a teasing tone to hide her disappointment.

On the screen, Krista glowed. "Yes. Blake is waiting for me upstairs. Talk to you again next weekend?"

"Sure. Tell Blake to call me on Monday. Enjoy."

"Oh, I'm sure I will." Krista winked. "Bye."

And just like that, Maddie was alone again.

Naturally.

CHAPTER SIX

Ang moh [ung maw], n. – In Hokkien: Caucasians. It literally means "red hair."

Aidan glared at the crowd of partygoers who stood between him and Madeleine, the sole reason he was here at the clubhouse of Sentosa Golf Club at three pm on a Sunday. Patrick, his brat of a godbrother, he could take or leave. But Madeleine he wanted to carry off to somewhere they could be alone. In his fantasy place, it would only be the two of them with no ringing phones calling them to work, no people to socialize with. There, they would be kissing, having sex all day and all night long, like they did in the Philippines. That had been the plan this weekend if he hadn't been summoned by the ambassador and if she hadn't had to meet Patrick before taking him on as a client.

They'd arrived at the game together before Patrick teed off at nine thirty this morning. But after constant phone calls from the embassy and his discomfort at having his back exposed to so many people, he'd decided to leave the course altogether. He'd only returned to pick up Madeleine and take her home with him, even though he knew she could go by herself.

Looking at Madeleine across the ballroom, he doubted she wanted to be on a deserted island right now. Surrounded by admirers, she was in her element. Although she'd told him of her contempt for Patrick this morning before they'd left to watch him play,

Madeleine didn't show it. She stood beside the golfer, laughing with him and allowing the arm he placed around her shoulders while they posed for photos.

If he hadn't known any better, he would think they were a couple. Their looks matched. Both tall and stunning, they shared the enviable beauty of those who possessed a multiracial heritage. Already, local news outlets were speculating on their relationship.

Aidan wanted to go over there and break Patrick's arm for touching what was his. To stake a claim on Madeleine. To say, "She's mine."

But she wasn't his—not yet, anyway. He'd thought last night was the end of his frustrations, but he'd arrived home to find an already slumbering Madeleine. Until they'd slept together again, he couldn't consider her his lover. It had to be tonight because he was leaving again tomorrow.

Aidan took a step towards Madeleine and Patrick only to stop short when he saw them speaking with a slick-looking man, their expressions intent on what he was explaining. The tableau didn't appear to be social. It looked like work.

Resigned to waiting longer, he walked farther into the room and chose a good spot to prop himself up. He understood and respected work. Like Madeleine had said, it was the reason they were both in this country. Even as yesterday's prisoner crisis had been resolved—they were able to connect the Vet with his family in the US and advise him of the due process in getting his name cleared of drug charges—more information had come in from various sources with regard to Aidan's main mission.

He was after a spy: a traitor who had been selling US military plans in Asia and Africa to various terrorist groups. With his background in cybersecurity and his attaché status, Aidan was uniquely qualified to follow a digital trail anywhere, even in the deep and the dark webs, and to conduct on-the-ground interviews at US embassies all over the world.

To many, Singapore was considered a cushy assignment, a reward after multiple hardship tours in the Middle East and the Horn of Africa. What they didn't know was that it was a very strategic location. This country was the ideal jump-off point to anywhere he needed to go to help build a case against the still-unknown individual.

His quarry was a slippery bastard, either an American, or a citizen of an allied nation. He was likely a diplomat who had been assigned to Singapore, Mauritius, and Aidan's next destination—Morocco.

Aidan had been enjoying the hunt until Madeleine arrived in Singapore. This week—today especially—he resented his job, and hers, for infringing on their time together.

He'd been patient, but he had to end nearly three months of celibacy. Today. For that to happen, he needed to take Madeleine home *now*.

On the heels of that thought, the Madison Avenue-type guy with them shook hands with Madeleine. Aidan moved to her line of vision when she looked around. The warmth in her expression the moment she caught sight of him was gratifying, as was her quick approach to his side. She'd forgiven his absence.

Aidan bent to kiss her cheek. She'd worn flats to watch the game, the sensible choice when one had to walk alongside the players through the course. "Ready to go?"

"Aidan," Patrick said from behind Madeleine.

"Hello, Patrick. Congratulations on the win." Aidan tipped his chin at the younger man.

He and his godbrother had never been close. Uncle Jack had often held Aidan up as the example for his sons to emulate. Ronan, the younger of the O'Connor brothers, had happily gone along, even so far as to call him *Kuya*, the Filipino address for older brother. Patrick had balked. He'd rebuffed Aidan's offers to help with schoolwork or anything at all. Aidan had had to give up. He had his own younger siblings to nurture. After Patrick's sulky behavior in New York during the holidays, their relationship had reached an all-time low, especially since Aidan placed himself firmly on Krista's side. Now, with Patrick's obvious crush on Madeleine, it could go even lower.

"Thanks. How do you two know each other?" Patrick asked, demeanor stiff.

"Aidan and I are dating," Madeleine answered, surprising him and Patrick, who gaped at both of them.

Pleased by her claim, Aidan placed a proprietary hand around her waist. Oh, yes. Goodbye, blue balls and cold showers.

"Small world, huh?" Patrick said, inanely.

"Tiny. Blake is a client, and Krista is my best friend," Madeleine declared, the last part in a warning tone.

Patrick regarded Madeleine for a few seconds before he spoke. "That's nice. You're practically family. Say hi to *Ate* Krista from me. I'll see you in New York in a couple of weeks. Aidan, great to see you again." He nodded to them in farewell and went back to rejoin the party being held in his honor.

"New York?" Aidan asked Madeleine a few minutes later while they waited for the taxi he'd called.

"For ten days in early February, plus travel back and forth. One week of conferences for new directors, and then a meeting with Patrick and his management team for brainstorming and strategy development," came the tired response.

"You'll be gone when I return, and I'll be away again when you come back." Their conflicting schedules were all kinds of bullshit.

She waited until they were inside the car before she asked, "Where are you going?"

Speaking in a low voice so the driver couldn't hear, he replied, "To Africa tomorrow, then to Thailand after that."

"Tomorrow? But that's too soon. We've barely seen each other." Madeleine's words and the plaintive tone of her voice reflected the frustration he felt.

"No shit," Aidan said under his breath. His annoyance was compounded by the thwarted desire to kiss her, to rev her up before they reached his apartment. He couldn't do that in public. Not here in Singapore, where they could be fined or even jailed for what he wanted to do to, and with, Madeleine. *Ang mohs*, or what the locals called "white devils," were prone to being accused of indecent behavior. As a diplomat, Aidan was expected to behave with the utmost discretion. Behave he would.

That didn't mean he couldn't touch. He left his hand on her thigh and took one of her hands to rest on top of his. The driver couldn't see, and Aidan wanted Madeleine to feel his desire. The moment they arrived in his apartment, he would pounce. He would ensure they both had a month's worth of memories stored after tonight.

He couldn't fucking wait.

CHAPTER SEVEN

Shiok [shauk], interjection – In Punjabi: something that provides extreme pleasure.

Hair fluffed around her head, eyes sparkling with anticipation, cheeks flushed from the steam, lips moistened by cherry gloss, Maddie declared herself ready. She'd primped, shaved, and buffed. Clad only in a red silk robe, she was all set to make love with Aidan again, after almost three months. "Oooh, yes."

With a delicate shiver, she opened the bathroom door. Her excitement dimmed. The bed was empty. "Huh. Why isn't he here?"

Maddie approached the bed and peered at the pillows. An indentation on Aidan's side told her he'd been there at some point. He'd turned on the lamps, which were now giving off a soft glow. "Ugh. He probably got a work call again." Surely if he'd gone out, he'd have knocked and told her before he left. That meant he was home.

She turned towards the living room, pausing by the threshold when she confirmed Aidan's location and activity. There he was on the sofa, typing away.

Maddie squared her shoulders. *Not tonight, work. You've had him practically the whole day. No more.*

Giving a sway to her hips, she stepped closer. "Aren't you coming to bed?" She perched herself on the arm of the sofa, deliberately letting the slinky cloth part to show off her smooth thigh.

Maddie sighed inwardly at the attractive picture Aidan presented. The day's growth of beard on his chin made her want to grab his face and rub it all over her body.

She couldn't wait to get him out of his clothes. He still wore his black Dockers and blue polo shirt, his definition of Sunday casual, from today's golf game. Maddie had catalogued his wardrobe when she moved in yesterday and concluded that the man only wore four shades—black, gray, dark blue, and white. No color anywhere. Ties were blue or gray. Socks were white or black. Cotton undershirts were white. Suits were unrelieved black, not even pinstripes. There were no jeans, no t-shirts with nasty sayings. He had white briefs, plain cotton, boring, staid. *He dresses like a grandpa.*

Like the elderly, he was also hard of hearing. "Aidan, did you hear me?"

He didn't look up from his computer, but he raised his right hand with the index finger pointing up.

"One what? One second? One minute?" What kind of response was that? He had been as eager as her to have sex. In the cab, he'd put his hand on her thigh, heating her entire body with the contact. The second they'd arrived in the apartment, he'd pressed her against the closed front door and proceeded to kiss her senseless. When they'd come up for air, she had spun away, telling him she needed freshening up. That was …

"One hour, Madeleine," Aidan said, his voice and his expression hard chips of ice.

He was pissed, with good reason. She'd done it again. She'd made him wait for her.

"I've cleared my inbox and written two security briefings in the time it took you to freshen up." Aidan closed his laptop and placed it on the coffee table.

No! He could *not* refuse to make love to her tonight. He was leaving tomorrow. They weren't going to see each other for an entire month.

Maddie rushed forward and straddled his lap as he started to rise. The sudden action pushed him deep into the sofa. "Don't go."

He bucked, attempting to dislodge her. She grabbed his shoulders to hold on.

She was getting steamed at his unyielding adherence to some arbitrary schedule. "Be very sure what you're turning away here, Aidan," she said when he stilled. "You should know by now I cannot have sex when I'm sweaty and stinky. If I took time getting ready, it was for our mutual pleasure."

He stared at her, unspeaking. His eyes roamed over her face and down to her heaving chest, to her enlarged nipples poking against the silk, and lower still, to her open thighs. To where her parted robe exposed her naked lower body, her bare pink sex. He kept his gaze there for so long, she squirmed, flushed all over. Beneath her, his cock hardened, twitched. When he raised his eyes to meet hers, the ice had thawed.

Voice dark and husky, Aidan gritted out, "You, Madeleine Duvall, are hard work." He planted his palms on her naked butt and pulled her flush against his erection before toying with the sash at her waist. "Lucky for you, I'm not afraid of hard work. The fulfillment that comes with a job well done is worth it." His fingers tugged at the ties to no effect except to tighten the knot even more.

Buoyed by her success, Maddie placed a hand on top of his. "Let me." She eased off him slowly, grinding her hips on his thighs before standing between his spread legs. "Get ready to put in some overtime, Colonel Ryan." With a sultry smile, she shrugged the silken garment off her shoulders and shimmied until it pooled at her feet.

"It will be my pleasure, Ms. Duvall," Aidan drawled, moving to the edge of the couch and encircling her waist with his arms.

Maddie moaned her pleasure when he rubbed his stubbled cheek against her belly, exactly like she'd imagined. She closed her eyes and soaked up the sensations as Aidan's big hands roamed all over her body. As he rediscovered her dips and valleys, got reacquainted with her curves and planes.

Her body heated and chilled. Warm where he had touched her and cool where he had not, except the place where she could feel his hot breath. Between her legs, dampness coated her flesh. The scents of vanilla and the musk of her arousal rose to perfume the air.

She opened her eyes and looked down. He was staring at her. *There.* His hands on her butt pressed and squeezed rhythmically.

Small waves of pleasure rippled through her when his right hand moved slowly from her back to her hip, the palm surprisingly calloused. It hovered over her pubis, not quite touching, yet tingles pulsated all the way to her chest.

In Makati, Aidan had been a thorough lover, but never this excruciatingly deliberate. He was making her pay for her tardiness.

"Aidan ..." she breathed. Her voice husky, she barely recognized it as her own.

"*Sssh*. I'm working hard here."

"Do something." An involuntary whimper escaped her lips. Her nails dug into his broad shoulders. If not for his shirt, she'd have left marks there.

He didn't look up, but his lips kicked up at the corners. *He's enjoying making me beg, the sadist.*

"Like what?" Aidan moved his other hand to bracket her hips, and his thumbs met in the middle. And pressed. "Like this?" The digits separated, parting her nether lips as they descended. "Or this?" He dipped one thumb into her liquid heat. It slid up and pressed the swollen nubbin of flesh that indicated her readiness.

Maddie's breath came out in a rush as she watched him bring his thumb to his mouth.

Looking up, he sucked on the digit, lips enclosing it totally, seductively. There was no gray in his eyes now. Deep blue and bright, they affected her with feverish heat.

"Sweet Madeleine, you feel good. Look good ..." Aidan made a show of licking his lips. "You taste good." Dark promise filled his voice.

She swayed towards him. Her knees couldn't support her anymore. His grip on her left hip tightened, catching her. Then he got to his feet, taking forever it seemed. He lifted her as if she weighed as little as a down pillow. Maddie's legs curled reflexively around his back, and her head nestled in the crook of his neck as he strode into the bedroom.

With more care than he had shown her since they'd reconnected, Aidan laid her down softly onto the massive bed. His hands caressed her until he let go to straighten, his eyes never leaving hers. In sharp contrast to the torture he'd put her through, he made quick work of his clothes.

His tattoos now revealed, Maddie gazed in appreciation at her warrior lover. The US Air Force motto and symbols decorated his chest—Aim High. Fly. Fight. Win.

Right now, Maddie aimed her sight low, on his swollen cock rising proudly from a nest of neatly trimmed hair. On his balls, which hung heavy between his wide-spread legs.

Turnabout is fair play. She lay back to take her fill of his male beauty, looking where he was one hundred percent male.

Is he flexing? The vain man.

Maddie raised a slim leg into the air and circled her foot in command. "Turn around."

Aidan's eyes flashed with humor at her dominatrix tone. Eyebrow raised with promise of retribution, he intoned, "As you wish, Mistress." He raised his right hand to his temple and after a sharp salute, turned in a perfectly executed military about face.

Maddie's lips quirked at Aidan's temporary compliance. She looked forward to the punishment he planned to mete out later, but for now, she would play to her heart's content.

"At ease, soldier."

With an indignant shake of his head and a muttered, "Airman," Aidan obeyed. He parted his legs and clasped his hands at the small of his back. Nothing in his pose screamed ease—head forward, shoulders back, spine and legs straight—but her officer held it easily. He had been doing it for nearly half his life; it had become second nature.

Aidan's bearing was so much a part of him, as was his pride of his heritage. His back was inked with his Irish clan's family crest: three white griffins on a red background, with the Gaelic clan motto *Malo mori dam foedari*. He'd told her it meant "I would rather die than be dishonored."

Gorgeous. Absolutely divine. Maddie sighed in admiration. She got on her knees by the edge of the bed and reached out to touch the tight globe of her man's ass. Intent on her mission, she didn't see the hand that shackled her wrist before she could reach her target.

With his hand still cuffing her wrist, Aidan turned around and presented his spectacular front to her view again.

Maddie raised her eyes slowly, past the ridges of his abdominal muscles, pausing to admire his smooth hair-free chest. She continued her perusal of his corded neck, square jaw, his stern unsmiling mouth, aquiline nose, until she finally met his stormy blue eyes.

"Inspection over, Mistress?" The words were subservient, the tone anything but.

"Not yet, Airman. And call me General," she responded, pulling him closer using her manacled right hand as leverage. He allowed himself to be tugged forward.

"A thorough inspection requires the use of the five senses." Maddie's gaze roamed all over his body again before locking eyes with him. "Sight, check." Without taking her eyes off his, she enclosed Aidan's hard cock in a tight grip, eliciting a harsh groan from him. "Touch and sound, check, check." Bringing her head closer to his penis, she made a show of inhaling deeply. "Smell, check. Clean and musky. Piquant, yet sweet."

She slid her hand down Aidan's length, the flesh warm and steely beneath her palm. Seemingly lost to the sensation, his hold on her other wrist loosened. Maddie took advantage, her free hand joining the other to grasp her lover's manhood. Both were not enough to cover him completely.

In a hushed, reverent tone, she breathed out the final sense, "Taste," and wrapped her lips over the broad head.

***

"Fuck," Aidan exhaled. His body was hers to command. It moved according to her directions. His fingers dug into her sumptuous hair; his hips thrust in rhythm with the suction of her lips on his dick.

One more minute. He would allow Madeleine one more minute of control. Her mouth felt heavenly, but he craved thrusting into another hotter, tighter cavern.

Aidan's whole body jerked when the beauty before him changed angles and swirled her tongue along the sensitive skin beneath his cock's head. *Too much. Too good.*

He bent down and held Madeleine's jaw still, his thumb on her cheek. "Enough, Madeleine. Open."

The maddening woman did the exact opposite, hollowing her cheeks and swallowing around his cock, her throat holding him captive for a second. Aidan closed his eyes, gritted his teeth against the pleasure, and willed his body not to explode in her mouth.

He succeeded. Barely. In part because the vixen decided to retreat and let him go, but not before licking the pre-come that seeped from the tip of his sex.

He opened his eyes to see her sitting back on her haunches, hands on her thighs, a self-satisfied smile playing about her plumped-up lips. He met her gaze and she licked her lips like the kitten she portrayed so well.

"Lie down, Madeleine." Aidan retrieved a foil packet from the box of condoms he'd bought on Monday. There hadn't been a need for it until her.

"On your front. Head down, ass up." He tore the wrapper and suited up. In blatant disobedience of his order, Madeleine looked over her shoulder at him with a smoldering want. He dragged his gaze lower. Between her legs, her fingers toyed with her clit, rubbing, pinching, spreading her wetness around. "Starting without me, Madeleine?" he chided.

"Enough with the preliminaries, Aidan. Give it to me hard and fast. Now. Or else I will leave you behind." Putting words into action, she thrust two fingers into her depths.

This. Aidan grinned, stroking her plump ass. No coyness, no pretenses. "Not a chance, kitten," he countered as he plunged into her waiting heat. She didn't need to order him to go fast. He'd blow after only a few strokes, his balls were drawn up tight, ready to explode. "Hang on. We'll get there together," he promised as he pumped his hips with no rhythm whatsoever. He was too far gone, and so was Madeleine. Her inner muscles clenched on his cock, squeezing, drawing out his come.

Bending, he grasped a fistful of hair to bring her face around. To join their mouths in a kiss as deep and as lusty as their joining below. Her long moan of pleasure came out only a tad earlier than his groan of satisfaction. They pulsed and shuddered. They got there. Together, as he'd promised.

Madeleine flopped on the bed, face buried in the pillow, back rising and falling with heavy exhalations of breath. Aidan followed, blanketing her body with his.

"Round one," he murmured. She'd gotten her "hard and fast." The next one would be slower.

Being inside her was all his fantasies fulfilled. They fit perfectly together. If not for the condom, he'd have kept their intimate connection. Reluctantly, he withdrew and strode to the bathroom.

When he returned, Madeleine lay on her side, staring at him. Honey-colored hair spread out on the pillow, lissome body curled with sinuous grace on top of the rumpled sheets, plush lips turned up in a satisfied smile, she looked the part of a sexually sated lover. His. Officially.

Still naked, he climbed onto the bed, and lay down facing her. "Stay," he said.

Madeleine's brilliant eyes flashed. "I'm not a dog," she said, without much heat.

Aidan fought a smile and lost. "No, you're not. You're a beautiful woman." He placed a hand on her hip and gave the generous curve an affectionate squeeze. "Stay here while I'm gone." He'd obtained the ambassador's approval for an extension of her stay in his apartment past ninety days. "Be here when I return."

Madeleine reached out to stroke his chest. "Okay, but I still need my own place to escape to from time to time. Maybe I'll stay here during the workweek, there in the weekends. I'll call the realtor tomorrow and tell him I'm taking the East Coast flat."

Aidan gave himself a mental high-five. His scheme had worked. "That's probably wise," he said, pretending he hadn't expected her to insist on having a space to call her own. He'd spotted Madeleine's streak of independence from miles away. "I'm sorry I won't be there to help you move in."

"That's all right. I don't have much to move, anyway. I will leave most of my stuff here. If I need anything, I'll buy it new," she said, almost absently. Her focus was on his body, hand wandering all over, fingers poking at hollows and creases, nails scratching at raised scars. Like he'd done earlier with her. Reacquainting, memorizing. Heating him up again.

Aidan clasped her hand before it reached his groin. He pushed her gently to her back and leaned over her. "Madeleine, are you hungry?" he asked close to her ear. Without waiting for her response, he nibbled at her neck, mindful not to leave a mark.

Beneath his lips, her pulse thudded in her throat. "No, I had an excellent meal earlier. It was long … thick … juicy …" she breathed provocatively.

Said meal hardened even more.

Fuck me. This woman turned him on like nobody else.

He parted her thighs and knelt between them. "Good for you, but I am famished." He pressed open-mouthed kisses over the skin of her belly, bypassing her breasts. Later, on the third round, he would lavish them with his attention. This time, he had other plans. "You don't mind if I … satiate my hunger, do you?" He met her eyes over her mound, his lips a breath away from his early dinner. From a soft, warm, and creamy confection.

Madeleine raised her hips, offering herself. *"Bon appétit."*

No question about it. He would enjoy this meal. So would she.

CHAPTER EIGHT

Kena [can ah] v. – In Malay: a passive auxiliary; to suffer from some affliction.

Maddie kicked off her flats and fell face down on the bed in her East Coast flat, grimacing as she bounced on the hard-as-a-block-of-wood mattress. "Ugh! I should really replace this soon." The business class seat on the plane was softer than this extra-firm plank. She turned onto her back with a long, drawn-out groan. Everything hurt. Her head pounded, her shoulders ached, and her feet—her already-huge size-nine feet—felt swollen twice their size. She'd have lifted them to check if they looked normal, but she was too tired to even make the attempt.

A massage. How sorely she needed one right now. The tiny Chinese auntie from the spa in Novena would get those knots out. The treatment would hurt so bad, but it would feel so good afterwards. Yes, she'd schedule that. Tomorrow. For now, she'd lie on this uncomfortable bed and bemoan her dateless Valentine's Day.

One would think living with a man meant there was somebody to celebrate Lovers' Day with, except apparently for Maddie. Aidan was somewhere in Thailand, attending a multi-nation exercise weirdly named after a snake. It was only his second day, nine more until she saw him again.

She missed him. Except on days she was traveling, they'd chatted daily—a surprise to her, for

Aidan wasn't a big talker—before he went to work and after her meetings were done. A few minutes, nothing more. "Just checking in. Hi. Hello. Still alive. Busy." It was boringly normal, but it thrilled her. It reminded her that she belonged in a relationship. Yeah, she missed him.

Turning to her side, Maddie reached for her purse and took out her phone. Ten in the evening. That meant nine pm in Thailand. *Should I—*

It rang with a video call request. Aidan!

Sitting up to prop herself against the pillows, she pressed accept. "Hey."

"Hey." Aidan's image appeared on-screen, brows knotted. Concern etched his face. "You okay? You look tired."

Not a very flattering thing to say to your lover, but then, so like Aidan to be forthright. She *was* tired. That it showed didn't surprise her at all. "My flights were a nightmare. The first from New York was cancelled. Its replacement got delayed, needing a mad dash to the next terminal for the second leg, and on top of it all, the airline lost my luggage during a minute layover in Paris. My checked-in bag didn't make the connection to Singapore. It won't arrive until tomorrow."

"Ouch!" He winced. "At least, you're inbound. It would have been worse if it was the outgoing trip."

"Look at you, Mr. Glass-Half-Full," she teased, her mood lightening with his sympathy.

"Bah. I hate flying commercial. I don't like putting my life in another pilot's hands, but it's a necessary evil." He adjusted a pillow behind his head. "So, Paris. Did you see your father?"

Maddie's papa was currently stationed in the French capital, awaiting his next embassy assignment, and they'd agreed to meet when she transitioned between flights.

She thought back to her conversation with her father at the end of January, when she'd called to set up that quick rendezvous. She'd informed him she couldn't visit him this year because of her new job. He'd sounded so angry, she'd volunteered to change her flight schedule so that they could meet. Even then, his voice had been brusque, and he'd complained about her not making time for him. What a drama king.

"No. That was the mad dash part. The cancellation and the delay of the first two legs screwed up my itinerary. I didn't have time for a stopover. We managed a garbled phone call when I was already in the air. He said he's coming to Singapore sometime this year. Perhaps April or May."

"Why do you sound surprised?"

Of course he'd read that in her voice. He must be good at interrogations. "He's never visited me before. I was always the one who went wherever he was assigned," she said with a shrug.

"He's never been to the Philippines? Your friends have never met him?" Aidan asked, making her father sound like a loser.

"Never, ever." Except for Krista, no one had met her mother, either.

"Hmm. Did you say anything about us? You said you'd tell your friends and family."

Gulp. "I didn't have time. When he calls to confirm his dates, I will let him know." Maddie wasn't looking forward to that conversation. Her father would hate Aidan. Who was frowning on the screen.

"You don't talk regularly?" he asked in that disapproving tone again.

Maddie's knitted eyebrows matched Aidan's. "No. We e-mail. I call when I'm about to go see him," she snapped. So her family was dysfunctional. Not everyone was as perfect as the Ryans. Krista had gushed about them during the first conversation they'd had after returning from New York. Maddie had been envious. She'd never been invited to meet a boyfriend's family. That would be another level altogether.

"Are you going to introduce me?"

The inquiry jolted Maddie; it coincided perfectly with what she was thinking. Her elation fell upon seeing a tension in his shoulders. "If you're here, sure. Why? Are you nervous about meeting him?" She didn't believe that for a second. Aidan had to be one of the most confident men she'd ever met.

The raised brow told her what he thought of her question. "I'm sure I could take him in a fight if he's overprotective of you and disapproves of me. He's what? Sixty, shy of six feet, robust because of the wine and cheese he imbibes daily."

Maddie blinked at the accuracy of his supposition. "How did you know? Have you met him?" Her suspicion arose along with her tone. "Did you have me investigated?" She knew nothing about dating a military man, apart from what she'd watched in movies.

"Madeleine, that's a requirement. You have access to a high-ranking American military officer. Of course you'll be vetted," he said, brows meeting in the middle. "As it happens, they haven't started your security background check yet. You need to fill out some documents and schedule an interview. I'll ask my staff to provide you with both a hard copy and a fillable PDF file."

There he went again with the non-answers. Pressing fingers to her suddenly throbbing head, she muttered, "Thanks for the heads up, Colonel Ryan. Maybe when you come back, you can give me a thorough briefing of what's expected of me."

"Noted," he bit out tersely. After a moment of intense scrutiny, he spoke again. "When do you plan to go to the Tanglin apartment?"

"Sunday night. I'll stay here in the East Coast during the Chinese New Year weekend. It's closer to the festivities at the Marina Bay. Why?"

"I had something delivered for you there. For tonight."

"Oh. For Valentine's?" *Hmm*. That was actually quite sweet. This guy confounded her at every turn. "Is it something that wilts or melts?" She brought the phone closer, hoping to see a clue in his face.

His grin and the mischievous gleam in his eyes revealed nothing. "You won't know until you go and get it, will you?"

"Aidan!"

"Happy Valentine's Day, Madeleine. I have to sign off. I need to be awake at oh-dark-hundred hours tomorrow. If I don't get to talk to you over the weekend, *Kung Hei Fat Choi*." He waited for her to wave goodbye before he clicked off.

Maddie sighed, sliding down to lie on her back once more. Now that her conversation with Aidan was over, all her aches and pains had come back.

Guess I have to go home now, don't I? She couldn't complain. The bed in the Tanglin flat was better, anyway. The mattress was softer, and the sheets smelled of Aidan. The heady combination of scents from his soap, shaving cream, and deodorant was an aphrodisiac to her. One sniff, and she was ready to crawl all over Aidan and lick him from head to toe. Slowly. Especially the middle part of him; she loved lingering there.

Her temperature spiked just thinking about his body, lean and fit, not overly muscled but hard. His skin wasn't smooth all over. He dismissed the ridges on his back as bullet scars, but she loved touching him anyway. Her hands reached for him but found only air.

Maddie groaned. Her battery-operated boyfriend was also at the Tanglin place. She'd need it while she waited for her flesh and blood lover to return. She needed it now, damn it. Nine more days. Good thing she'd bought extra batteries before she left for New York. Even if she wore them out, there was a Cold Storage or the Market Place nearby. She'd survive.

For right now, as a short-haired American singer once crooned, it would just be her and her hands tonight: a lavender bubble bath, a couple of pain relievers, and self-love. Not a bad plan.

CHAPTER NINE

Lah [la], slang – In Singlish: a discourse particle that doesn't change the meaning of the sentence, just the tone. Also, *leh, liao, mah, siah*.

A droplet of water wobbled and shimmered for a long second before sliding down the tall leaf, catching on the edge, then, almost reluctantly, falling to collect on the red petal of a ginger flower. Had it rained before she'd ventured into the middle of this one-acre ginger garden? That was unusual for February, Singapore's driest month, but why else were the leaves so vibrantly green, and the flowers so stunningly colorful? How else could the air smell so pungent, sharp, earthy, and oddly sweet?

Maybe it wasn't rain. Maybe her senses were heightened simply because she was happy. Maddie smiled widely, uncaring that people at the neighboring tables in the restaurant at the Singapore Botanic Gardens were staring. She sniffed her wrist, one of the pulse points upon which she'd sprayed the vanilla scent made specifically for her by a perfumer in Paris. *Aidan gave me La Madeleine!*

She'd planned to go to the downtown apartment on Thursday after retrieving her bags from the airport, but that took a while to sort out, so she'd suffered another night in her East Coast flat. The complex was half-empty when she'd arrived. Many of the residents had gone on vacation for the Lunar New Year holidays. With no work and no relatives to visit,

Maddie had decided to pass the time at the Gardens before she could call Aidan and thank him for his gift.

If she hadn't just returned from a hellish trip, she'd have gone to Manila for the long weekend to visit her friends and consult with Blake and Krista on their wedding. Receiving this gift from Aidan more than made up for the disappointment, both for the lost opportunity and for his continued absence.

Maddie raised the menu to cover her silly grin. She couldn't believe her tightwad boyfriend had bought her an extravagant bottle of her favorite perfume. Okay, maybe tightwad was a hyperbole. Frugal more like, as evidenced by his act of turning off the refrigerator and the air conditioning before he'd left. She'd turned everything back on and re-stocked the perishables before coming here.

Aidan lived simply; he didn't have a lot of material stuff. His clothes and shoes were off the rack, not handmade. The branded items in his wardrobe were likely gifts from his brother Blake. The Hermes tie, the Hugo Boss shirt, the Ferragamo shoes—nothing was flashy. They were all understated in his favorite shades of gray and blue.

But for her, he'd paid hundreds of dollars, perhaps a thousand, for he got her a year's supply. The perfume was the least expensive part of the package. The crystal glass container was a work of art in itself, but the shipping cost had probably made Aidan wince. Still, he'd bought La Madeleine for her because he liked her scent, because he liked her. If he didn't, he wouldn't have asked her to live with him.

"Hi! May we join you?"

Maddie brought down the menu to stare at the couple smiling charmingly down at her. The petite, fair-complexioned woman wearing a short, red cheongsam, and her bald-headed, alabaster-skinned companion in a white muscle shirt and jeans both looked familiar. Where had she seen them before?

A quick glance around told Maddie that the pair could have sat anywhere they'd wanted. The viewing deck only had a few diners. Locals were most likely at home celebrating the first day of the lunar year. Those who considered today just another day on the calendar and tonight's dinner just another meal, sat inside the air-conditioned dining room, probably to take a respite from the heat, which was still high even now, in the late afternoon.

Returning their smiles, Maddie pointed to the chairs across from her. "Please."

As if choreographed, the two separated and sat on both sides of her.

Huh. Now we look like a mini version of The Last Supper. A multiracial one. The three of them faced the rest of the restaurant like their picture was going to be taken. Maddie had picked the corner table, intending to be inconspicuous. She'd attracted attention anyway.

Once seated, the woman held out her hand to Maddie. "*Xīn nián kuài lè!* I'm Hui Min Johnson. My husband, Kalvin, is Colonel Ryan's OPSCO."

"And I'm Noir Khan, husband to the embassy's press officer. We live in the same building as you. Hullo, neighbor," he said in a plummy accent.

With her Singlish enunciation and fast cadence of speech, Hui Min was Singaporean. Noir, from his accent and features, was British-educated Middle Eastern, Maddie guessed as she shook both hands. "Hui Min, Noir, it's nice to meet you. Happy New Year. Please call me Maddie."

Neighbors—that explained the familiarity. She'd seen them before, probably in the lift or in the pool.

On second thought, she probably hadn't seen Noir in the pool. Judging by his pale skin, he preferred the indoors.

"If you're wondering about Noir, his real name is Anwar," Hui Min said.

"Oh. I thought it was an ironic nickname like 'Tiny' for a hulking guy. Or, his partner is black who goes by the name Blanc," Maddie said, attempting to match the pair's friendly demeanor.

Noir rolled his head along with his eyes. "He is black! I wish he'd play along, but no. He prefers Nate. Boring!"

Maddie smiled at the joke. The affection in Noir's voice belied the complaint. He sounded very much in love with his husband. They seemed like a fun group; she wouldn't mind getting to know them better. "Are your husbands joining us later?"

Noir shook his head. "Not mine. We're just marking time until they return from dragon boat racing. We saw you and decided to introduce ourselves. We've been curious about you since the moment you moved in. Even more so when you disappeared, then showed up again," he explained, admitting their nosiness.

Maddie liked the candor. She usually didn't bother getting acquainted with nosy neighbors, but these two were changing her mind.

She turned to the local beside her, wondering how she celebrated her culture's New Year traditions. While yesterday's eve was the busiest day of the festivities, the following three days were jampacked with activities as well. "And you and your husband?"

"Kalvin and I will go to my parents again later for more *hongbao* distribution to the kids. *Alamak*, Chinese New Year making us *pok kai leh*," Hui Min said.

Maddie knew what a *hongbao* was: a red envelope you put cash into for gifts during weddings or birthdays. The other words were still unfamiliar to her.

"Sorry. *Pok kai* means penniless." Hui Min answered her unasked question.

Her confusion probably showed in her expression. Now was a good time to ask about the other acronyms they'd thrown around earlier. "You said he's an OPSCO? What does that mean? Is he Aidan's supervisor?" She knew Aidan had a high rank but not how high.

The two exchanged looks before Noir patted her hands, which were resting on the table. "Darling, how long have you and Colonel Ryan been together?"

Despite her caution about talking to strangers, Maddie blurted out the truth, "Less than a month." She wasn't counting the weekend fling in the Philippines. They hadn't been "together" then.

"Only? Wah, you have a lot to learn *siah*. Good thing we're here to help," Hui Min claimed, rubbing her hands together in excitement.

Help? She hadn't known she needed it. Of course, anything to do with Aidan Ryan *had* to be complicated.

"But first, let's order." Noir was already waving to a server even as he uttered the words.

"OPSCO stands for operations coordinator. My husband is the chief of staff for the Defense Attaché Office," Hui Min explained the moment the waiter had left with their orders. "At the moment, Colonel Ryan is the senior defense official here in Singapore. The title usually goes to the ALUSNA— the naval attaché—not the Air Force officer, but we don't have one at present."

"Because of Big Ken." Noir dropped the moniker with aplomb, looking at her expectantly, as if she should recognize the name.

She did. He was a PR case study. "The American defense contractor married to a Singaporean who pled guilty to bribing Navy officials with money, prostitutes, vacations, and other so-called gifts to gain classified information. He and his cohorts defrauded the Navy and the United States of millions of dollars."

"Exactly. You're good," Noir gushed.

Maddie waved away the compliment. "Some of the recipients enjoyed their gifts in the Philippines. My agency had to prepare a crisis management plan for a hotel chain, in case they got implicated." Privately, she hid a smile. It was good to know about something that tied Aidan's job and hers together.

"Your guy is a big deal around here. The ambassador is a political appointee, not a career diplomat. And he relies heavily on Colonel Ryan for *everything*," Noir whispered, leaning close to impart the last statement, even though it was impossible for anyone else in the restaurant to hear.

For spouses, these two seemed fully informed about the happenings in the embassy. "Am I supposed to know all this? Is there a quiz I need to pass?" Maddie asked flippantly. "I'm just a girlfriend, and we're only starting our relationship."

She was with Aidan because of their mutual attraction, not for what his power or influence could provide. Her French passport allowed her entry to many countries, including the US, without a visa. The job she was good at gave her the means to obtain anything else she wanted. No, Aidan's high rank didn't mean much to her.

Hui Min snorted. "Who says so? Maddie, the last thing you are is *just* a girlfriend. You're a unicorn, the one who caught the Sexiest Man Alive, as far as the embassy staff is concerned. Colonel Ryan had to get the chief of mission's approval to have you live with him in quarters leased by the US government." She paused when Maddie gasped. "Not everyone gets approved. Most don't even try. Easier to live elsewhere *liao*. Even those who've been approved are only allowed ninety days, the maximum length of stay for Americans without a visa. In your case, there's no such restriction. If that doesn't make you special, I don't know what will *mah*."

Maddie's heart swelled. Well now, that was a nice perk. Aidan had never let on that he'd had to jump through hoops for them to live together. He'd made it sound like he'd barely exerted any effort. She thought he'd wanted her with him, and he'd got it at a snap of his fingers. But he hadn't.

"How do you know all this?"

"I work at the embassy. I'm an office management specialist, fancy title for a personal assistant," Hui Min replied. "More importantly, I'm the ambassador's OMS," she declared proudly.

Maddie's jaw dropped. That explained the insider knowledge. "Are you allowed to give me this information? Isn't it confidential?"

"It's not classified top secret *lah*, and I'm not broadcasting it to the public. I'm only telling it to you," Hui Min said, leaning away, her friendly demeanor gone.

"Thank you, Hui Min. I didn't mean to sound accusing. I just don't want you to get into trouble." Maddie patted the other woman's hand. This was only the second overture of friendship she'd received in this country, and while she treasured Rini at work, she could use the companionship of other people outside of it.

"Don't worry. No problem one," Hui Min assured her. The other woman's gaze sharpened. "Know what? It's great you're cautious about what's secret and what can be shared. It'll do you good in the future with Colonel Ryan."

Maddie schooled her features to not show her disquiet. Her and Aidan's number one rule of honesty was in jeopardy. He could always hide things he considered top secret, like where he'd been in Africa and how he knew what her father looked like. She didn't have a similar shield to hide behind.

She gave Hui Min a nod, then turned to Noir. "How about you? Do you also work at the embassy?" Here was another possible friend. In the Philippines, her looks and cultivated image didn't invite many. If not for her college friends, she'd have no one. Now, she appeared to have three.

"Sort of. I'm a yoga instructor. I teach there once a week," he replied. "And your man, the deliciously divine Lieutenant Colonel Aidan Ryan, is my best student, whenever he shows up for class. He hasn't been in since mid-December, but when he's there, he's awfully distracting. Darling, he's so bendy! But I'm sure you know that already," he said with a wink.

Heat suffused her face. Oh, yes. Bendy. And strong. One time, during their sex fest before he'd left for Africa, Aidan had taken her standing in the middle of the living room at their apartment. He'd held her up with her legs over his arms, her bottom clutched in his hands, while he'd thrust in and out of her. She'd come so hard, she'd been out of breath. He'd been barely winded, had demanded another orgasm from her and had gotten it, as he always did.

"That good, huh?" Noir teased.

Maddie groaned and buried her flaming face in her hands, which elicited laughter from her companions.

"Okay, okay. We'll stop teasing. Our food's here anyway," Noir announced.

"Thank you!" Maddie greeted the server with more enthusiasm than he'd probably expected. She reached for the bluefin tuna tartare and heirloom tomato salad she'd ordered before he could place the plate in front of her.

She wasn't overly hungry, but she needed to process all this unexpected information. Maybe with their mouths full, her newfound friends would stop probing her personal life. But she also wanted to know more about being in a relationship with a military guy, apart from adjusting to his constant absences. He had more power than she'd imagined, which meant there were a lot of secrets he couldn't share with her.

This opportunity was too good to miss—she'd be a fool if she didn't seize it. Madeleine Duvall was no fool.

CHAPTER TEN

Steady [ste dē], adj. – In Singlish: attached (in a relationship).

Peace washed over Aidan the moment he entered his apartment at half past three on Saturday morning, twelve days after he left it for a regional exercise in Thailand. *Home at last.* He breathed in deeply, replacing the odors of people, junk food, and jet fuel with the scents of hearth and woman. He carefully set down his duffle bag on the floor, strode to the bedroom, and followed the perfume of vanilla.

He stood beside the bed, content for the moment to simply look at Madeleine's perfect form. Her perfectly nude form. She slept on her stomach, her back bared to the waist, the red silk sheets pooled around her. It was as if she were posed by a painter. The faint illumination from the living room lent her smooth skin a golden glow. Too pale; she might not have gone to the beach at all while he was away. Except for the day after her return from New York on Valentine's Day, she hadn't stayed at her apartment near the beach park. She'd remained here, as he'd requested before he'd left.

Still wearing his flight suit, he'd come straight home after parking the plane at the Paya Lebar Air Base. He and his team had done a short debrief while they waited for air space to clear at Bangkok's Don Muang Airport. More debriefing would follow in the coming week. He approved wholeheartedly of the time saved, for it allowed him to rush home. To Madeleine.

He sat to view her closer, to smell, to feel.

Madeleine had filled out some since her arrival in Singapore, probably from all the chicken rice she had been eating. His lips twitched at the remembrance of her blatant lie during their first lunch here in the city. She'd claimed to have been eating rice since forever. Not true. The pantry in her Makati apartment hadn't contained any rice, and when they had eaten out, she'd only ever ordered salad with meat or fish.

Aidan nudged the blanket aside, revealing her completely. *Aaah, there it is.* Her magnificent ass. Round and toned, the globes invited his touch. He obliged, extending a hand to stroke and caress. Her skin was warm beneath his hand, soft and unblemished.

Light as a feather, his hand continued its exploration, down the slope of her butt, the crease where it met her thigh, past the back of her knee, until he reached the tattoos on the outside of her right ankle: an "M" glyph with its arrowed end entwined with the tail of a scorpion, the symbol of their shared Zodiac sign.

Everything he'd read about Scorpios held true for Madeleine: direct, brilliantly sharp, sexy, and incredibly loyal. She was also stubborn and secretive. He prided himself for having all those qualities; it was no wonder they were drawn to each other from the start.

"Aidan?"

The husky sound of Madeleine's voice saying his name went straight to his groin. He yanked off his boots and lay beside her. She wiggled to nuzzle against his neck.

"Hi, honey. I'm home," he said against her fragrant hair, resuming his caress of her skin.

"Were you copping a feel while I was sleeping?" Madeleine was, herself, burrowing her hand inside his uniform to pat his chest.

"I was. Am I not allowed?" He lifted his hand off her. In the Philippines, they hadn't cared for permission, often waking the other with kisses.

She paused her exploration to reach back and return his hand to where his fingers had been, tracing circles on her bare ass. "Of course you are, silly. I thought I was dreaming."

"So, you dreamt of me, huh? Was it X-rated?" He'd jacked off to the visual of her lying naked on his bed, just like the picture she'd presented tonight.

"Pornographic. What else would it be? Have you met us?" was the sassy response.

He tugged her hair with his other hand. "You have a point."

Like a cat, she rubbed her head against his hand. "Hmm. I always do."

Again with the "always" that wasn't true, but he'd let it pass. Since she was wide awake now, he had another thing he wanted to discuss. Raising his left hand, he tilted her chin to meet his gaze. "Thanks for decorating the place. It looks great." He'd only had a glimpse of the living room when he came in, but he'd seen rugs on the floor, prints on the wall, table runners, multi-sized vases, and decorative pillows on the sofa. None of that had been there before he left for Thailand. Madeleine had been busy.

"You're welcome. I enjoyed shopping for the pieces."

"I'll bet you did. Let me know how much everything cost. I'll reimburse you."

"No need. I'm keeping them after ... you know."

After they broke up. A cheerless thought. "Regardless, I'd like to share in the expenses. They must have cost you a pretty penny." The stuff was classy; it looked expensive. "I'm sure you also decorated your place on the East Coast."

"I did. Don't worry about it. I can afford it."

Aidan had no doubt she could buy the whole damned store if she wanted to. His Madeleine was loaded. Her condo in the Philippines, now occupied by Krista, was huge. Her shoe collection was massive. She'd had that Porsche and she currently possessed the fancy title of Regional Director for Southeast Asia. He would bet her salary exceeded his. One day, maybe he'd know exactly how much she earned. But only if she volunteered the information. He wouldn't invade her privacy like that. He could, but he wouldn't.

When he'd done the background check on Krista—he liked her, but he had to protect his brother, didn't he?—Aidan had also looked up Madeleine. Not too deeply: only what was available online, which was plenty. She was a model and a public relations professional, after all. What he'd found out about both women had reassured him. If necessary, he could dig deeper. But, not yet.

"Why are you still in uniform? Are you going back out?"

"No, I arrived only a few minutes ago and came straight to bed."

"Do you need help getting undressed?" Without waiting for his answer, she sat up and straddled him. She reached for the zipper and pulled it down.

It was oh-dark-hundred-hours, closer to dawn than midnight. He was exhausted, but what did one do when one had a hot, willing woman on top of him, intent on ravishing him? He lifted himself off the bed so she could take off his constricting clothes. He felt grungy but if she didn't mind his plane stink, he wouldn't point it out. She was the one who cared about smelling fresh before having sex. He didn't.

It felt too good to have her kissing him, touching him everywhere, especially where he ached the most. This time, he'd let her take the lead. Tomorrow, he'd return the favor. Tenfold.

***

Maddie locked eyes with Aidan as she slithered down his body. She both felt and heard his sharp intake of breath as she rubbed her breasts against his tattooed chest. Felt, too, the hardness of his erection poking at her belly. She planned to pay attention to it, eventually. For now, she'd take advantage of his mellow mood and relish his distinctive masculine flavor.

Opening her mouth over his nipple, she lightly bit down on the distended flesh. Aidan's eyes narrowed, the only indication that her bite affected him at all. *Nothing, huh. How about this?* Maddie flattened her tongue and licked the part she'd bitten. She tasted the salt of dried sweat. With any other man, this would have turned her off. For some inexplicable reason, Aidan's filth only enhanced her desire for him. It was madness.

She turned to his other nipple and gave it the same treatment, all the while, watching his face for signs of impatience. There were none. He'd closed his eyes, but the faster than normal beat of his heart against her cheek and the stiff column against her stomach told her he had not fallen asleep. Yet.

Perhaps it was time to hasten this process. She'd been aroused since the first touch of his hand on her body. It had taken all of her will not to moan at his caress. When he'd stopped at her feet, she couldn't help herself: she'd pretended to wake up. With what she had in mind, he wouldn't have to pretend to be awake.

Raising herself to straddle his thighs once more, Maddie grasped Aidan's cock with both hands and positioned it at the entrance of her body.

His eyes flew open, gaze zooming in between her legs before looking up at her. "Are you sure?"

"Yes, I'm on long-term contraceptives, plus, I've had my tests done and they were negative."

"Mine were too."

"I know," she said before plunging down to engulf him in her heat. Bracing herself on his chest, she leaned forward to kiss him. She slanted her mouth against his and sipped at his lips. "Welcome home, Aidan," she whispered before straightening again and setting a steady rhythm of advances and retreats.

Her dreams fell short of reality. Of the thickness and length of his cock, unhampered by latex, inside her. Of the living, breathing man to which it was attached. Of the perspiration dampening her skin as she climbed to the peak. She couldn't go there alone. They had to reach it together.

Grinding her hips to take him deeper, Maddie entwined her hands with Aidan's. "Come with me."

"I will. I'm with you. Take your pleasure. I'll have mine when you do."

With those words, he unleashed her restraint. Her moans mixed with his grunts as their passion built to a fever pitch. She came with a muffled scream, her pleasure so intense, she almost blacked out. As promised, he joined her in ecstasy only a few seconds later.

Boneless, her muscles loose, Maddie collapsed on top of him. She had to clean up, but languor was stealing over her body. Aidan made such a great bed, firm and soft at the same time. She'd just close her eyes for a minute. For sure she'd wake if he moved her. "I'm glad you're finally home, Aidan," she murmured into his chest.

"Happy to be home, Maddie-mine."

Had she heard that right? He'd called her Maddie. And his.

As he should: he was hers, after all.

CHAPTER ELEVEN

Kaya [ka ia], n. – In Malay: a jam made from coconut milk, eggs, and sugar: popular in Southeast Asia.

Maddie-mine? What kind of sentimental crap had gotten into him? Aidan pumped his legs faster, glad for the sparse early Saturday morning traffic on Cluny Road, right outside the Botanic Gardens. Tanglin and Nassim roads were far too busy to let his mind wander while running, but here was fine. With only the occasional car passing by, the air here was fresh and perfumed by the trees and blooms from the nearby gardens.

He had to admit that last night—this morning, more like—was special. Their first sex without the use of a condom was the only physical thing that had changed, but the feelings were different. They were more enhanced, somehow. That Madeleine could make him erect with one touch was nothing new. That she'd fallen asleep immediately after their mutual climax was familiar as well. She'd barely stirred when he wiped away the traces of their lovemaking from her body.

Aidan scoffed at his own thoughts. There he went again with the tender shit. Lovemaking. He hadn't read a romance novel since high school, yet here he was spouting hearts and rainbows.

Maybe he could blame having survived a near mid-air collision on the last day of the exercise in

Thailand for the sappy sentiments. Nothing like almost dying to make a man feel the need to celebrate life by fucking. Except it was more than that now. In Makati, yes, it had been pure lust, nothing else. Here, in Singapore, they'd started to form a bond.

Granted, they'd only lived together for two days before their respective trips, but through their daily video chats, especially since her return from the US, he'd gotten to know Madeleine better. What he'd learned, he liked. She was excellent at her job, as proven by her promotion and as he'd observed during their conversations. On more than one occasion, she'd remarked on what certain famous personalities should have said and done to avoid controversy or to recover from a scandal.

She was extremely loyal, always taking Krista's side whenever the engaged couple disagreed on a wedding detail. The one time Aidan had supported Blake, Madeleine had clicked off on him. Aidan chuckled now at the memory. A couple of pedestrians gave him a wide berth, but he didn't mind them. Madeleine delighted him, and that was that.

He was glad she'd started making friends, with his OPSCO's wife and his yoga instructor, no less. Madeleine had told him they'd hung out when he was in Thailand. They'd gone swimming regularly at the pool and dragon boat racing one time at the Kallang River. It pleased him to see her form attachments with people connected to him. He didn't want her to be lonely. With him gone all the time, she needed companionship. He couldn't think of anybody better than Hui Min and Noir. The former, especially, would be a good resource for Madeleine if she wanted to know more about being in a relationship with an active duty service member.

For his part, he had to deal with the very public aspect of Madeleine's job. He'd have to rein in his jealousy every time she was photographed beside an attractive celebrity, like Patrick. Madeleine would never betray him. Her extreme loyalty applied to him now.

Her loyalty to her family made him wonder. Madeleine had been tight-lipped about them. She'd only ever mentioned a diplomat father, who sounded like a douche from the little Madeleine had told him. Why had he never visited his daughter in the Philippines? They hardly ever talked, except to arrange an annual meet-up.

The concept of once a year was alien to him. If he missed a weekly check-in with his mother, he was sure to receive a reprimanding voice mail from Giulia Ryan within twenty-four hours. To not have the support and love of his family was unthinkable.

Madeleine was thirty years old and from all indications, she liked being in a relationship with him. Still, part of him wondered why she hadn't told her father about them yet. Didn't she think he would approve? Huh. It didn't matter. She'd agreed to undergo a background check so they could continue to live together. That was good enough for him.

Aidan slowed to a walk. A once-a-year father, a distant mother, no siblings, no close relatives—perhaps, that explained why Madeleine chose the type of work that had her surrounded by people all day long.

Why she'd accepted his offer to stay in his place. Madeleine hated being alone. *Well, she isn't alone now. She has me.*

He stopped at the light at the corner of Cluny and Napier, wiping sweat off his forehead with the back of his hand. At almost nine, the sun hadn't reached its summit yet. It was warm but still pleasant. This area in particular, with its abundance of trees and adequate distance from commercial establishments, provided a comfortable living environment. This was likely the reason why many of the embassies were located here, with his own just up ahead.

Although it was quiet and empty now, his workplace still put Aidan on high alert. He let out a derisive snort. As if he could defend anything in his present sports attire, with no weapon except the phone strapped on his left upper arm.

The Marines could protect the embassy—that was their job. His, for now, was to go home and prepare Madeleine for her visit to the regional security office this week. It would not be fun: necessary, but not something one enjoyed doing.

After a quick check of his pulse, Aidan decided to take the stairs. He was barely winded after his five-mile run.

He was on the ninth floor when the piercing wail of a fire alarm stopped him in his tracks. His head jerked up. Madeleine had still been in bed when he left an hour ago. He had to get her out.

Fear more terrifying than the near air collision he'd experienced yesterday thrummed in his chest, sending his heart beating double time. He raced up the remaining flight of stairs to the tenth floor, skidded to a stop on the landing, and forced himself to calm down, to think rationally.

He was reassured by the absence of smoke coming from the apartment. The air smelled fresh, too. With a shaking hand, he felt the knob. It was cold. *Thank fuck.*

Releasing a breath, he inserted his key and pushed the door open in time to hear the chirp of the fire alarm a second before it was silenced. "Madeleine!"

"In the kitchen. I'm fine. No need to bellow."

Faint smoke lingered in the air, and steam fogged the microwave door from the open pot of boiling water on the stovetop. The charred remains of what he presumed was formerly bread on top of the open garbage can confirmed his suspicions: Madeleine had tried to cook and failed miserably.

Muttering to herself in a mixture of French and Filipino, she stood at the counter with her back to him, cutting the crusts off another couple of slices. The set of her shoulders and the straightness of her spine told him she was determined to conquer this task.

Her casual disregard for what he perceived as danger meant that setting off the fire alarm was a regular occurrence. No wonder she only ate salads and raw foods. She wasn't a good cook. Neither was he. Good thing they were compatible in many other ways.

Aidan waited for her to set the knife down before speaking. "Madeleine." He couldn't hold back the hint of laughter in his voice. "I leave you for an hour, and you try to burn down the building? That won't look good on your security check."

The glare she threw at him over her shoulder would have shriveled his balls if she hadn't looked so sexy in her tank top and boy short panties.

"Your toaster is a piece of shit," she spat at him even as she placed more bread into the accursed appliance.

"It's old and cheap. I haven't used it in a while. It must be rusted. What are you cooking, anyway?" A couple of eggs in a bowl, an open jar of something greenish, and softened butter sat on the counter. *Kaya?*

"*Kaya* toast," she confirmed, without looking away from the toaster.

"You don't eat white bread, egg yolks, butter, or jam. Is that for me?" *Well, now. Isn't that thoughtful?*

Madeleine grunted, which he took as an affirmation. She peered into the toaster, then pressed the lever to expel the barely browned bread. With grave ceremony, she transferred the slices to a small plate. "Success!" She held up the tongs and whirled around and around in a dance of joy.

Catching her in mid-twirl, Aidan pressed her to his chest and kissed her laughing mouth. "Congratulations." He couldn't help the rush of affection. She looked adorable, celebrating the accomplishment of such a simple task. "Thanks for making me breakfast."

"Hmm. Rough," she remarked, rubbing his stubbled cheek.

It didn't sound like a complaint. She remained in the circle of his arms, her head on his shoulder.

"And sweaty."

Okay, that last one was said with a wrinkle of her nose. Aidan knew he stunk badly. His last shower was at a hotel in Bangkok, more than a day ago. Releasing her from his hold, he said, "Fine, I'll shower. I can take a hint." He dropped a kiss on her forehead before stepping back and heading to their bedroom. When he was safely out of missile range, he tossed over his shoulder, "The fire extinguisher is under the sink, by the way."

The expected growl and the epithet about his nether region followed him all the way to the bathroom.

Delightful. *I'm keeping her.*

***

Addresses, employment information, relatives, foreign contacts, seven years' worth of travel destinations and people encountered, financial record—just some of the things she had to provide the US government.

"*Aaargh!*" Maddie leaned forward on the couch to drop the forms onto the coffee table. If she could rip them up, she would, but she'd already answered some questions, and she didn't want to rewrite them. "Remind me again why I said yes to living with you?" she grumbled to Aidan, who was lounging on the sofa across from her, sipping coffee while reading a book on his e-reader. He was more relaxed than she'd ever seen him.

He'd devoured the breakfast she'd made in mere minutes, obviously starved after his run. Eight pieces of toast slathered with *pandan*-flavored coconut jam and a thin slice of cold butter, two soft-boiled eggs, and *kopi o kosong gau*—a strong brew of Malaysian coffee without sugar or milk. She'd bought the ingredients from a *kopitiam* near work the other day, knowing he enjoyed the local meal.

There wasn't a Singaporean dish Aidan didn't enjoy. The local breakfast dish was the only thing she was confident enough to try. Except for the first batch that she'd scorched while tending the pot of boiling water, Maddie thought she'd done great for a non-cook. And this was the thanks she got: having to reveal all the details of her life to the government of a country she wasn't a citizen of.

"You said yes to living with me because I asked nicely," was the response. "And the great sex."

If she was being honest, Maddie had to agree. After she'd fished for the invitation, Aidan had asked nicely. And, yes, the sex was excellent.

She'd brought this upon herself, not knowing what it meant to be coupled with an American military officer before parking her stuff in his apartment. According to Hui Min, it meant an entire forest had to die to produce paperwork for both the State Department and the Department of Defense, so she could stay with Aidan for longer than three months. The ambassador's approval did not exempt them from having to go through the laborious process. The burden fell mostly on Maddie because she was the foreigner and Aidan had the top secret security clearance.

"We also agreed on staying together for at least one year. Have you changed your mind about that?" Aidan asked with a slight tension in his voice and posture. He'd put down his coffee and tablet and leveled his gaze on her.

They'd discussed that during one of their longer chats, along with possible causes of a breakup. Aidan had said he could think of only two reasons for them to end their relationship before their mutually agreed timeline: disloyalty and betrayal of trust. She'd agreed with him.

"No." Her answer was accompanied by an emphatic shake of her head. "I haven't." They'd already burned through one month being in two different countries. Physically, they were more compatible than ever. Emotionally, they had a lot of catching up to do. Staying together for a long period of time was the answer. "So, these forms are telling me that being with you is like holding a national security position, is that right?" She wanted to return the room to its earlier lighthearted atmosphere.

It worked. Aidan relaxed again. "Or like a spouse," he said, with a glint in his eyes.

Maddie gulped. Her heart skipped a beat.

Madeleine Duvall-Ryan: it rolled off the tongue perfectly. Maybe they could have a double wedding with …

No. Too soon. She could not allow the picture of Aidan and her in formal attire—she in red, Aidan in his dress uniform—saying their vows to each other to crystallize in her mind. It was too presumptuous.

"A spouse? For real?" she croaked, reaching for her lemon water to ease the sudden dryness in her throat. No, that wasn't longing in her voice. Definitely not.

"As good as, without the ceremony and your lack of entitlement to healthcare benefits and claim on my retirement," Aidan said in the manner of someone quoting an official handbook.

Maddie pulled a long face. In a high-pitched voice, she cried out, "Oh, no. Two things I really need you to provide for me. What am I going to do now?"

"You might have to sell one of your shoes," he said gravely.

"That's a hard no for me." She stood. "Bye, Aidan. Great knowing you." She waved for effect, smiling widely.

His face held an answering smile, but his expression quickly turned solemn again. "Seriously now, Madeleine. Are you having a hard time with this? I've been undergoing these investigations for most of my career; I'd forgotten how exhaustive they are the first time around."

Maddie sat. "I know this is a necessary procedure to make my living here official. I've got nothing to hide. I just didn't realize how much work I have to do in order to complete these forms." She eyed the papers with disgust. "I have dual citizenship in France and the Philippines, my father's in Paris with his fourth wife, my mother is in Sydney with her current boy toy, my four stepsiblings from her two former husbands are all over the world, and I travel for work practically every month. Have done so for the past five years. And as far as the US is concerned, *all* my contacts except for you and Blake are foreign." Reeling all those things off exhausted her.

"Did you receive the forms the Tuesday after Chinese New Year from Hui Min? I'll give her grief if she sent it late."

"I got them, but I'm not even halfway through yet. I managed to put in my residences, education, and employment history." She'd copied that stuff off her resumé. "I do have a job, you know. I can only work on this in the evenings, as I can't take them out of the flat," Maddie reminded him.

Aidan held both hands in the air. "I know. What do you need me to do? I can't help you gather all that information. It's personal to you."

"Can you reschedule the interview?" she asked.

"How much more time do you need?"

If she filled in the travel information this weekend, she'd knock off the worst of the work. "I'll get my financial report from my accountant on Tuesday, so another week."

"All right. I'll fix it on Monday."

"Thank you." She sagged on her seat in relief.

"Now, will you relax and tell me more about Madeleine …" he reached for her French passport "… Estrella Duvall? Your middle name is Star? It suits you."

He'd been freer with the compliments lately. "Thanks. You know that's my mother's maiden name, right?"

"Yes, I've heard of the Filipino convention of giving names from *Tita* Belen and Uncle Jack. Your mother's maiden name becomes her and your middle name once she marries." Aidan picked up a sheet of paper with her notes. "Irene Estrella Williams Gibson. She doesn't have Duvall listed here. Weren't your parents married?"

"No, I was illegitimate and didn't have an entry for 'Father' on my birth certificate. I used Estrella until Jean-Marc Duvall acknowledged me, when I was sixteen. I started using his surname professionally soon after, and then had my name changed legally when I officially became a French citizen."

"How did that happen?" Aidan probed.

"I started modeling when I was fourteen. Became semi-famous after I was paired with a popular Hollywood actor in a television commercial. My face was on the cover of an in-flight magazine, and that's how my father discovered me. According to him, I look like his *maman* when she was young, only darker." She laughed at the irony.

"What's funny about that? Surely your grandmother was a beautiful woman."

"I wasn't laughing at that. It was the fact that many things about my life have to do with flights. My mother was a flight attendant. That's how she and Papa met. On a plane."

"And now you're dating a pilot. We also met on a plane."

Maddie let her thoughts drift away from the paperwork. Taking advantage of Aidan's talkative mood, she made herself more comfortable on the love seat, raising her legs and tucking them beneath her. "Yes. Good thing I like flying."

"Why didn't your father know about you? How come it took sixteen years for him to acknowledge you as his daughter?"

"I was a product of a one-night stand. Here in Singapore, actually. My father was a consul at *l'Ambassade de France.* He and my mother started flirting during the flight and finished it in her hotel room. Usual story: contraceptives didn't work. She never saw him again after that night. He told me he was assigned to the Middle East soon after. She claimed she didn't know she was pregnant until she couldn't fit into her uniform anymore." Maddie remembered, at age twelve, angrily confronting her mother about the issue of her paternity. She'd been told to be happy she was born at all.

"So, you grew up without a father," Aidan concluded, his expression soft and sympathetic.

Maddie took a deep breath and let it out slowly. They were getting into heavy territory here. She hated talking about this part of her life, but Aidan was engaged, intent on knowing more about her. If he wanted to see her, scars and all, without him running away, she'd show them.

"I grew up without my birth parents. After delivering me, Irene—that's what my mother insisted I call her—left me with her only living relative and went back to work as soon as she could. My true mother, the one I called Ma, was Irene's sister, my *Tita* Cel." Fresh grief beset Maddie at the memory of the most wonderful woman who'd ever lived. "When she was alive, she was the one person who put me first, even before her own interests." Tears filled her eyes and streamed down her cheeks. Sobs came out when she tried to talk. She still missed her Ma.

Wiping her face with her palms, she jolted when strong arms lifted her and enveloped her in their warmth.

"I'm very sorry, Madeleine. When did she die?" Aidan stroked her back. His sympathy eased her sorrow.

"Nearly thirteen years ago. Just in time to see me graduate from high school. Breast cancer," she told him, sniffling as more tears flowed. "She was the reason I had to work so young. Irene supported us financially, but it wasn't enough to pay for Ma's medicines and treatments, on top of basic necessities. Ma encouraged me to accept my father's belated recognition. I didn't want to, at first. Finances were tight, but we were managing. That's why it took over a year before Papa and I met in person. Ma knew she didn't have long to live, so she wanted me to have at least some semblance of security, even if only a financial one."

"Your father came through for you?"

"He did, big time. Papa petitioned for me to be granted a certificate of French nationality and sponsored my annual trips to see him wherever he got assigned. He paid for my education so that I could stop modeling altogether. I still accepted jobs through college—I didn't want to be entirely dependent on him—but I had the freedom to choose which ones to accept. Before, I couldn't afford to turn down any projects I was offered. I needed every one of them.

Weirdly enough, the more I turned down offers, the more in demand I became."

"And Irene?" Aidan probed, his voice coated with disdain.

He already disliked her mother based on her words alone. How loyal.

"Was relieved that she wasn't obligated to support me anymore. She sends gifts on my birthday and Christmas, and we have a meal together when she's in town, but that's the extent of our contact. It's better that way. If we spend more time together, we fight." Maddie had never met a more selfish woman than her biological mother. She'd long vowed never to be like Irene. If she married, it would be for keeps. If she had children, she would keep them and shower them with all the love inside her. "Krista, *M'amie*, and my papa are my family." And now, Aidan too. But she couldn't tell him that. Not yet.

"Do you resent having to mention your stepsiblings on the form? You obviously have no relationship with them." He tapped the same piece of paper he studied earlier. "Your notes here merely say Williams kids and Gibson kids."

"Yes, I don't even know their names. And the fact that their slim connection to me is through Irene makes me want to slap whoever created this questionnaire." She bared her teeth at Aidan in mock anger. Her mood had lifted with his kindness and understanding.

"If you've never met them, you don't have to name them as contacts."

"I could kiss you for that." She blew him one.

"I'll collect later," he promised. "Your father doesn't have any other children?"

"No. He gets married to have a presentable partner for all the parties he has to attend as a diplomat. None of them were mom material. The three I've met hated me. They resented having a grown woman for a stepchild. So, I'm his one and only offspring. That's why he spoils me."

"You're a daddy's girl."

"*Naturallement.* As I'm sure you're a mama's boy." She'd bet he was a cute kid—a little man at age two.

"Ah, but that's where you're wrong. Blake is Ma's favorite. Craig is Da's because he's practically his 'mini-me,' and Darcy, of course, is another daddy's girl like you. If I'm anyone's favorite, it's probably Uncle Jack's because I followed him into the Air Force."

Maddie leaned back to study Aidan's face. The statement was uttered matter-of-factly, with no jealousy whatsoever. She arranged herself on his lap so she could see his expression better. "It must be nice to belong to a big family," she said with not a small amount of envy. Krista would have that soon: family on both sides of the Pacific.

"Yes, it is. We fight, but we always know we can count on each other for support if needed. I'm luckier than most in that sense," Aidan said, his stern features soft.

Maddie's heart squeezed in her chest. *I want that.* She wanted him to talk about her with the same expression on his face, with tenderness in his eyes and a smile on his lips. What would it take? she wondered.

Not something that could be answered right now. She jumped off Aidan's lap at the sound of the clothes dryer's buzzer, indicating it was time to swap loads.

"I'll get it. Continue working on your paperwork. Maybe you'll be able to finish earlier than you think," Aidan suggested, already walking towards the washer and dryer in the kitchen.

Ah so, he's right. Their arrangement was indeed as good as being married without the official papers. She cooked, and he washed the dishes. They planned to do groceries later.

What next? Ba—.

No. Not going there yet. Not at all.

CHAPTER TWELVE

Blur [bler], n. – In Singlish: clueless; in a daze; unaware of what's going on.

Aidan wanted to retract his previous week's declaration to Madeleine that it was great to belong to a big family. Right now, in his living room, looking at the live video images of Blake in the Philippines and Craig in Thailand on his laptop, he wanted nothing more than to bash his brothers' heads together the next time he saw them. They'd been talking crap about his and Madeleine's living arrangements since they came online a couple of minutes ago. Blake, two years younger and the more polished version of Aidan, with curly hair and cleft chin, was humming the wedding march. Craig, the youngest but largest Ryan son at six feet five inches, had quickly offered to cater their imaginary reception.

"Don't look too worried, A. I'll give you a discount. All you have to do is pay for the ingredients." His brother, the James Beard Foundation award-winning chef, casually waved off his thousands of dollars in fees.

"Me too. You can honeymoon at Perlas or Paraiso," Blake chimed in, naming his exclusive resorts on the islands of Boracay and Palawan in the Philippines. "But not this December; that's *my* wedding. Not before then, either, if you want Paraiso. It won't be finished until November."

His siblings amused Aidan, but it was his duty to be the hard-ass eldest. He gave them the middle finger salute.

"You're no fun, bro. I think you might have been adopted," Craig teased. "Everybody else in the family has a sense of humor except you."

"You're both marginally intelligent guys," Aidan said. "How could you make the leap from living together to getting married that quick?" He was genuinely interested in what his brothers thought, particularly Blake.

"You're thirty-six years old, A. You've eluded capture in more ways than one since you attended officer's training. Until now. Of course we're jumping to conclusions," Blake said reasonably. He didn't say *duh* or roll his eyes, but both were implied. "Where's the lovely Maddie, anyway?" He looked beyond Aidan's shoulder as if expecting her to suddenly appear. "Why are you home alone on Friday night? Trouble in paradise already?"

"She has an event tonight. A new car launch." Aidan glanced at his phone to check for updates on social media and saw her posing with a group of people he determined had to be clients. In his opinion, she was more alluring than some of the professional models there. With her signature pose of left hand on her hip, chin up, and perfect teeth showing, Madeleine drew all eyes to her, of that he was sure. Tonight's smile, though, was a tad forced. Maybe even pained.

"Finally found someone who works as much as you do, huh?" Blake observed.

"You should know. You're one of those demanding clients who make her work past regular office hours and on weekends." Aidan pointed a finger at Blake, indignant on behalf of his girlfriend. She hadn't been able to complete the security check paperwork this past week, despite the extension he'd obtained. Preparation for tonight's launch had occupied all her time.

Madeleine hardly ever complained about work. About people, she did, but not the projects. He could tell she loved her job, but he'd seen her exhaustion whenever she came home from an overtime session. While he was in Thailand, she'd overseen a couple of events that had gone past midnight. They hadn't talked the previous night, so they'd done a quick check-in the morning after. She'd had bags under her eyes and had yawned so much that her words had been muffled and unintelligible.

"Hey, don't blame me. My activation events are in the daytime and during the week. Now, more than ever, my evenings and weekends are sacred," Blake countered, his features softening. "I'd rather spend them with Krista."

"Why aren't you with Maddie tonight?" Craig butted in.

"I hate those things. I only go if it's mandatory. I hadn't even gone to all my medal awarding ceremonies." He'd only gone to those he had felt he'd deserved the medal for, like the Combat Action Medal from Iraq, and the Silver Star from Afghanistan. He had nearly died there, covering a visiting brigadier general's six. Damn right he'd gotten his stinking medal.

"So, she did ask you and you declined," Craig guessed.

"Madeleine mentioned it last night. Said she had to work late today, and if I wanted, I could go and meet her there. I didn't commit either way." He shrugged. "I don't like making small talk and being gawked at." He'd had a taste of it during the golf champion's party for Patrick, and he didn't care for it at all.

"But you're expecting her to be fine with being put on display during your military balls," Craig argued.

"It's not the sa—," he started to say, then thought better of it. It was exactly the same. The embassy had scheduled three formal events this year, and he expected Madeleine to attend them with him. He planned to show her off. It was entirely possible she wanted the same of him.

"Too late now," he said, glancing at the clock at the base of the screen. Nine o'clock. The event had started at seven. "It'll be over soon. I'll go next time."

"Make sure you make it up to her. Tonight, not later. When she gets home, apologize for not supporting her," Craig advised.

Craig had been in a long-term relationship with a Thai woman who was one of his sous chefs in his Los Angeles restaurant. She'd died last summer in a wildfire that had gutted their restaurant, and Craig had brought her remains to her parents on Koh Samui. He'd returned to the US for the Ryan's annual Christmas family reunion, but he'd gone back to Thailand as fast as he could.

Blake drew Aidan's attention to the left side of the screen by nodding. "Agree. You have to be careful to keep the balance, bro. Maddie can't be the only one giving in all the time."

Stung, Aidan glared at him. "That's a foul, Blake. You know nothing about what goes on here," he snarled. There were risks in cohabiting with Madeleine. If they were accused of living together under the guise of a lawful marriage, his chances for a promotion could be jeopardized and his pay cut.

"I know you, big brother. And I've known Maddie far longer than you have. She's a proud woman, yet she's living in your apartment when she is given an allocation by her company to rent one on her own. I can see her personal touches all around you. I'll bet she paid for those decorations out of her own pocket and didn't let you repay her."

Mentally wincing at the accuracy of Blake's observations, he fumed anyway. "Madeleine has her own fully furnished place near the airport," he bit out. "I didn't force her to stay here with me. She always has a choice where to go every time she leaves work." That she'd always chosen to come to his apartment made him inexplicably happy. "If you think that Madeleine allows me to dominate her, then you don't know her at all."

Blake held up both hands. "Dude, I only want to give you a reminder not to go too alpha on her. Of course I know Maddie can hold her own." He nodded.

"She's Krista's best friend. She's *my* friend. I'm looking out for her."

"You're whipped, B," Craig joked in an attempt to break the tension that had slipped into their conversation.

"Nah. Just in love," was the smug retort.

All three of them had witnessed the way Krista's quiet strength had matched Blake's stubborn will in New York during the holidays. There *was* a balance there. Blake spoke the truth, Aidan acknowledged in silence.

Madeleine *had* given him more than he had to her, especially financially. True, he paid for their food, but as he ate the larger share, it was only fair that he had that responsibility. The perfume had cost over a thousand dollars, but that merely equaled the value of one of the five prints on his wall.

He was humbled by his live-in lover out-earning him. He'd never encountered that kind of situation before. His experience had been the opposite. Women called "tag chasers" had pursued him because of his military benefits.

"Aidan, don't brood. You'll do fine." Blake, the smartass, broke into his thoughts. "If you follow our advice."

"When did you resign as CEO to become a relationship coach?" His little brother was having too much fun lording it over him in the matters of the heart. "Where's the lovely Krista? What are you doing home alone on Friday night? Trouble in paradise already?" he asked, throwing Blake's earlier questions back at him. Craig chuckled on his side of the screen.

If it was possible for Blake to look even more self-important, he accomplished it. Puffing out his chest, he declared, "She's on a girls' night out with her squad, *M'amie*. What did I tell you? Balance, bro. Balance."

"Smug ass," Aidan muttered under his breath. He addressed Craig. "What about you? Why are you not doing dinner service tonight?" He'd been surprised to see his youngest brother online. He'd taken advantage of the opportunity to include him in the chat.

"I traded shifts with my *chef de cuisine*. I was going to contact you before you suddenly showed up online. I … um … wanted to ask you something." Craig scratched his beard, a faint flush coloring his cheeks.

"What's up?"

"I'm going to Singapore mid-July for a food festival and the awarding of Best Restaurants in Asia. We got in the top ten, so the hotel is sponsoring my fare and my stay, but only for the duration of the event. I want to sightsee a little …"

"You want to stay here?"

"If I may. Money's tight. I'm well paid, but I'm sending support to some of my former staff. The insurance company is still dragging their feet about the settlement for the fire." Craig's blue eyes narrowed in anger.

"I understand. I'll have to ask Madeleine first, though. This is her home too." They also had to clear the guest bedroom of her stuff. He didn't know how they were going to do that. She'd bought more clothes and shoes and accessories in the six weeks since she'd moved in.

"You've always been a quick learner, big brother. Proud of you," Blake chimed in.

Aidan ignored Blake and angled his body to talk to Craig. "I'll let you know. When do you need the answer? I'm assuming soon, since you want to book the flights."

"Yup."

"Is tomorrow okay? I don't know how late she's coming home. I'll ask her as soon as I can. Will send you a text once I have the answer."

"That's cool. Thanks, A."

"You're welcome, C."

"Hey, what about me?" Blake complained.

"Goodbye, B," he and Craig chorused, grinning at each other.

***

Maddie closed the front door behind her as quietly as she could, not wanting to wake Aidan when it was past midnight. She didn't want to talk to him right now. Still, she was grateful he had left the living room lights on, so she didn't have to fumble for them in the dark. She turned both locks before stepping out of her heels and dropping her bag beside them. She'd pick them up tomorrow. Mr. Neat Freak would just have to deal with her clutter because she was too tired to put them away tonight. She should have been home by ten, but the account manager, who usually supervised the breakdown of the stage, had gotten sick in the middle of the event. Maddie had had to stay and do that, plus make sure the model car got back to the showroom.

The one thing she wanted—make that, needed—right now was the bed. The thought of her favorite piece of furniture hastened her steps towards the bedroom.

Maddie reached for the hem of her dress as soon as she entered. Her arms were too heavy to unzip it. The stretchy material lifted smoothly until it bunched beneath her chest and stayed there. She pulled and twisted. She shimmied and tugged. It wouldn't go past her boobs. It hadn't been this tight when she wore it last ... in December, maybe?

She should have changed into a looser dress when she'd struggled to zip it up this morning, but she'd been running late. Changing dresses meant she'd also have to choose a different set of underthings, and shoes and bag to match. So, yeah, she'd stuck to her bandage dress. Now it looked like she'd have to tear it to get it off.

"Need help?"

Maddie yelped, her startled gaze drawn to the bed where Aidan was sitting up, wide awake, openly laughing at her.

"I was enjoying the unconventional striptease," Aidan said, getting up to walk towards her. "But when I heard you threaten to rip this beautiful dress, I had no choice but to intervene."

In his white cotton t-shirt and gray sweatpants, Aidan shouldn't have made her mouth go dry with thirst or her knees to weaken, but he did. When he stepped behind her to lower the zipper of her troublesome sheath, it took all her strength to keep standing. The warmth of his palm on her neck as he moved her hair aside made her skin tingle.

Maddie didn't want to tingle. She'd nursed her anger at Aidan the whole night for not coming to her event. Rini had asked about James Bond again, and Pierre had been flirty. Her boss hadn't believed her claim of being involved, since she had no evidence to support it. No pictures to show, no man beside her. After six weeks of being with Aidan, she still wasn't his top priority. It rankled because he was fast becoming hers.

But her resentment was melting away. This seductive welcome home seemed to her an apology. He was taking his job of helping her disrobe seriously, stroking his hands over her shoulders and down her arms, her sides, her hips, taking the dress off with lazy deliberation. As if he had all night. His big body curved over her back as he reached around her to push the spandex dress down her legs. When he straightened, his erection pressed against her butt.

A low moan escaped her lips. Her head felt too heavy; she lay it on his broad shoulder. She was weakening, readying, awash in heady sensations. He smelled so good, so edible. The tangy, woodsy scent of his soap mixed with the mint of his mouthwash tantalized her. *Hmm.* Maybe a kiss would be okay.

Ugh, no. Her breath needed freshening. The sour aftertaste of champagne coated her mouth, and her face had to be cleansed of makeup. She twisted away from his light hold and bent to grab her dress, careful not to brush any part of her body against his, knowing it would weaken her resolve.

"Thank you," she said formally. "You didn't have to wait up." On weeknights, he was asleep by ten. Later on Friday and Saturday, but still before midnight, except when he'd had to take a call from Washington, DC. Those disruptions made him growly and frowny, especially when they got him out of bed.

"I didn't," Aidan agreed, "but I wanted to." He reached for her hands, making her drop the dress and stand before him in her underthings. "I want to apologize for not going to your event."

Poof, resentment gone. "Why?"

"There's a reason I don't like crowds and being exposed, which I would have been in an outdoor event like tonight. I was shot in the back at a busy market during one of my deployments. I've avoided similar situations as much as possible ever since. I also didn't know how I could be useful to you while you worked."

The lump in her throat kept Maddie quiet. Her head bowed as shame coursed through her. In her self-absorption, she'd never asked why Aidan always kept his back to a wall. Why he never took off his shirt in public. Why he came to bed fully dressed. The explanation shook her. She found his scars sexy. To him, they were reminders that he could have died.

He squeezed her hand and she lifted her gaze to his.

"Madeleine, I didn't tell you this to guilt you. I should have said something the moment you invited me, instead of refusing to go."

He was being honest. She should be too. "I wanted more people to know that we're together. I know it's shallow but having you by my side makes me look good. Feel good. You're quite pretty to look at, you know, Colonel Ryan."

He laughed. "I will go next time you invite me," he promised.

Maddie nearly swooned. This was a different Aidan from the one she'd met in Manila. Even from the one who'd come to her office in January. She'd taken off her mask and shown him her true self. So had he.

"You look like him. You sound like him." She moved closer to sniff at his neck. "You even smell like him. But you're too nice. Where is my Aidan? The cranky, impatient, alphahole of yore. What did you do with him? Should I call the Marines?" She choked back a laugh at her last question.

"Smart ass," he returned, letting go of her hands and lightly tapping her butt to match his words. "Go do your nightly ritual before I forget that you've had a long day and throw you to the bed. Not to mention that you're probably cramping right now."

Maddie goggled at Aidan. "How did you ...?"

"Know that you're having your period? I took out the trash. I also have a sister with whom I'm forced to share the bathroom whenever I go home to New York."

"Oh, okay. So, you also know that ..."

"We can't have sex. Yes. You've told me before, you don't like the mess. But that doesn't mean we can't fool around in other ways."

"It doesn't?" She didn't know. None of her former boyfriends had been interested in seeing her when she had her menses. She'd always been too crabby—bitchy, even. To avoid unpleasantries, she'd often cited work as an excuse for not going out on a date. Now, she couldn't hide anything.

Aidan turned her around gently in the direction of the bathroom. "I'll be happy to show you," he whispered, dropping a kiss on her shoulder, "as soon as you change into something more comfortable."

The seductive promise was all Maddie needed to make quick work of her nightly ablutions. No one-hour dawdling. She cleaned up and changed into a fresh pair of panties and pads.

The soft strains of her sleep music came on. *Hmm.* Odd choice for fooling around. It was mostly an instrumental new age type. Although, there was a sound effect on the playlist that she liked: the one of the sea waves washing over the shore. That sound, along with memories of her time at the beach with Aidan, had always stimulated her rather than put her to sleep.

Face flushed, heart racing, Maddie stepped back into their bedroom. Her excitement immediately deflated. On his side of the bed, reclining like a sultan, his hands behind his head, Aidan remained fully clothed. "Why aren't you naked?" she demanded. "I broke a personal record in getting ready, but I'm sure I gave you enough time to strip down to your briefs." Disappointment sharpened her tone of voice.

The crazy man just laughed at her, his wide shoulders shaking with his mirth. That was twice in one night.

"Now who's the cranky one?" He held out both hands and wiggled his fingers. "All I need. You'll see. Come here, my weary woman," he said, patting the mattress to his left.

She went. That was her side of the bed anyway. Assuming her usual sleeping position on her stomach, she waited for Aidan's next move.

He reached for something on the nightstand before getting to his knees and straddling her back.

"What are you doing?" Odd seduction technique, this.

"*Sssh*, relax. I'm taking care of you." He was extra careful not to put too much of his weight on her. They only touched along their thighs.

"Ooh," she moaned as his fingers combed through her hair, rubbing her scalp, easing her headache as he gathered the tresses to one side.

"Hold this," he ordered, taking her right hand from its position on her side to anchor the long strands to the pillow.

The moment the heady scent of vanilla infused the air, she knew what he was going to do. Just like that, all tension left her. The music made sense now.

"I bought this from your perfumer," he said as he spread the fragrant oil on her shoulders and all over her back. "It promises to soothe tired and sore muscles, promote rest and relaxation, and nourish your skin."

It was working. The soothing and relaxation part, at least. Maddie sank deeper on the bed as Aidan alternated the pressure and pace of his ministrations, digging hard and slow at the base of her neck and shoulder blades, while sweeping fast along the fleshy parts of her back and thighs.

He delivered on his promise to take care of her, sliding off the bed to better reach her entire body.

There was pain—was there ever. The tear-inducing force of the heel of his hand on her left calf, the jolt caused by his thumb on her right instep that had her gasping for breath, she'd expected all of that. It was part of the therapy.

She also anticipated the healing and the pleasure. Especially the pleasure. There was relief when he scratched the marks her tight bra had left on her flesh. Tingles fluttered on her skin from the glide of his palms on the sides of her breasts. The sly forays of his fingers beneath the waistband of her boy shorts generated liquid heat.

She wanted him to press on her mound. To turn her over so she could feel his touch on her nipples. Not merely his touch, but his mouth. His breath, his tongue, his teeth, his lips. "Ooooh," she moaned, unable to contain her shiver of delight.

Reading her thoughts correctly, Aidan rolled her to her back and promptly climbed atop the bed to straddle her hips. He was clad only in his briefs, as she'd expected him to be earlier, deliberately pressing his bulging hardness to where she was softest.

Aidan's voice was rough as he tipped the vial over his palm, catching the drops as they fell. "Did you know when you chose vanilla to be your signature scent that it's a powerful aphrodisiac?" He rubbed his hands together, warming the oil.

"Yes," she gasped as he brought his hands down to her chest, smoothing the oil in circular motions. Approaching, but never quite touching her nipples.

"That's why I can't keep my hands off you. The reason I can't get enough of your scent," he said, bending down, inhaling deeply. "Why I enjoy the feel of your skin, why I crave your special taste."

Words failed her. She sighed and moaned as Aidan's mouth closed over her left breast, then her right, laving and suckling, causing fire to flare within her.

His hands, his fingers wreaked havoc on her senses, but it was his cock that she wanted the most. The friction of it against her clit. He had to move.

She parted her thighs, nudged at his to spread wider, and found her voice to demand, "Lift, Aidan. I want you between my legs. I want to come." He'd brought her this far, he should see it through until the end.

Above her, Aidan shifted as instructed, smiling at her when she quickly raised her legs to encircle his hips. "Whoever associated vanilla with plain and boring should meet you," he rasped. "You're an original, Madeleine." Blue eyes gleaming with lust, he swooped down to cover her lips with his.

He tasted sweet and cool, of vanilla and mint, decadently delicious. Maddie couldn't get enough of him. She clung to his broad shoulders, ground her lower body against his iron-hard length, and clawed his fine ass. Her climax drew near. "More. Faster." She rocked, whimpered, pleaded.

He answered, and gave, and gave until she shuddered and came. Only then did he take his own pleasure.

Satiated and drowsy, Maddie pressed a kiss to Aidan's shoulder. They were both a mess—a sticky and oily and sweaty mess—but she didn't mind. It would be easy enough to wash it off. What she wouldn't wash off was tonight's new openness in their relationship.

Above her, Aidan shifted. She wrapped her limbs around him tighter. "Not yet," she whispered. He responded by rolling them to bear her weight. She kissed him again. Her Aidan was so considerate.

My Aidan. She'd called him that. Did he notice?

He once called her "Maddie-mine" but never repeated it. He still addressed her as Madeleine.

She liked the possessiveness from both of them. Tonight, she'd wanted to parade Aidan in front of the Singapore public and proclaim him property of Madeleine Duvall. In some ways, she was glad she hadn't succeeded. That would have been unfair to Aidan. He wasn't ready.

The day he claimed her publicly as his would be the day she knew he felt the same for her as she did for him.

CHAPTER THIRTEEN

Sekali [scar lee], adv. – In Malay: lest; what if.

"The Southernmost Point of Continental Asia," boasted the sign beside the suspension bridge Maddie and Aidan had just crossed. It linked the tiny strip of land to the white sanded Palawan Beach on the other side of the lagoon. The islet they stood on now also claimed to be Asia's closest point to the Equator. To Maddie, it felt more like the closest point to the sun with this early-March heat. Singapore's dry season was in full swing. Here, on Sentosa Island, the heat was thankfully alleviated by the breeze from the sea.

When Aidan had asked her during their now-customary weekend breakfast of *kaya* toast if she wanted to go to the beach, Maddie had agreed right away, thinking they'd go to her flat on the East Coast. Since his return from Thailand two weeks ago, she'd stayed at the Tanglin apartment the entire time, trying to finish the background check paperwork. She'd finally completed it last Sunday. After the phone interview this past Wednesday, they were done, officially cohabiting. Unless the investigator found something alarming about her information, which she doubted, as she'd never done anything illegal except for speeding, they were in the clear. This trip to the beach was a treat, a reward of sorts. Some much-needed vitamin Sea.

Maddie hadn't been to the beach since Boracay in November. In the Philippines, she'd have already gone to Balesin in Quezon and back to Boracay by this time. It was funny, really. The trip to Quezon took four hours, but she couldn't go to a beach in Singapore, a mere fifteen minutes away. In the case of her own flat, it was only a five-minute walk down the street.

Well, she was here now, wearing a wide-brimmed *sinamay* hat on her head, black shades perched on her nose, and an outfit—a turquoise spaghetti-strap top and denim shorts over a bikini the same color as her top—perfectly suited for the weather and location. To her surprise, Aidan wore equally appropriate clothing: a baseball cap, a soft dove-gray t-shirt, and navy-blue walking shorts.

"Is this okay?" Aidan interrupted her thoughts, pointing to a spot in between two dwarf coconut palm trees several meters apart. Their feather-shaped leaves provided some measure of shade. A handful of steps down a bunch of rocks would take them directly to Singapore Strait, the main body of water in the area. This close to lunch hour, few people loitered nearby. Most were at the food courts.

"Sure. Looks good." Maddie dropped her bag to the sand and pulled out a *sarong* printed with the colors of the rainbow. She spread the large cotton square out, kneeling in the middle to weigh down the corners with fist-sized rocks. Once she judged the cloth secure, she sat and beckoned Aidan to her side.

He sat facing the island instead of the water. Odd, but so like him. His position allowed him to see anyone approaching from three sides. Even now, he scanned the beach, for what, she didn't know.

She waited until his gaze fixed on her before talking. "This is a great idea. Thanks for thinking of it." He'd told her he didn't like being exposed, yet here they were, out in the open. He'd done this for her. "Why here, though?" There were six other beaches in Singapore, two of them on the same island where they sat.

"We haven't gone out in a while. I figured we could use a different scenery than our apartment. As to why Palawan Beach—I thought you might be missing the Philippines."

"Hmm." Aidan really *was* thoughtful. Both Siloso and Tanjong beaches were party central. Too crowded and loud for a relaxed visit. Most of Palawan Beach's visitors congregated on the lookout towers, suspension bridge, and children's activity centers, leaving the beach for serious sun worshippers like her.

"Are you? You haven't been back since December, right?" he prodded.

"Yeah, I do miss parts of it, especially my friends. Although we video chat constantly, it's not the same as seeing them in person." She gave a small sigh and shook her head as the next thought chased away the sadness. "I don't miss the traffic, though. That's one stress inducer I'm glad I don't have to suffer for a while."

"I don't blame you. How does Sentosa compare to your country's own Palawan Island?"

"I can't really compare. Palawan is huge. It is by itself an archipelago with nearly two thousand islands. You have to specify which island you're referring to: Puerto Princesa, Coron, El Nido, or another."

"Do you know exactly where Blake and his partners are building their new resort?"

"Paraiso is going to be at Isla Pasko, near Puerto Princesa, which is the capital of the province. Your *Tita* Belen's family owned it before they sold it to Blake and his partners. When did you last talk to your brother?"

"Two Fridays ago, when you had that car launch."

Aaah. *That* night. "Same time as your other brother Craig?" That must have been quite the conversation among the brothers. Aidan had asked her permission to have his youngest brother stay in their apartment. She'd fallen asleep feeling hopeful about a future for them.

"Yeah. He texted to say thanks again, by the way, for letting him use your apartment when he comes for a visit."

"I got it exactly for that reason: so our friends and family have somewhere to stay when they come to Singapore. My friend Angela is coming in June. Craig in July. Also, how can I turn down the promise of a home-cooked meal by an award-winning chef in return?"

He clutched his chest in pretend hurt. "My cooking is not good enough for you?"

With an answering smile, Maddie reached up to tap his nose. "You have many talents, Aidan Ryan, but cooking is not one of them. And, I'll have you know that preparing cold sandwiches is not considered cooking."

Aidan caught her hand and planted a courtly kiss on her knuckles. "Says the woman whose French card will be revoked for not eating butter or drinking wine."

"They can pry my French card out of my cold, dead hands." She honestly couldn't care less about the stereotypical French qualities people looked for in her. She was her own person.

"You're proud of that part of your heritage."

Maddie raised her chin. "I am proud of who I am, period. All the parts—Filipino and French, good and bad. I consider myself lucky. The fashion, advertising, and film industries, especially in the Philippines, are enamored of mixed-race talents. I took advantage of that. It served me well, particularly at the start of my career. I'd have missed out on many opportunities if I didn't look like this. It's unfair to a lot of people, but as they say, it is what it is. I didn't make the rules. I didn't break any by following them."

If he thought she sounded defensive, Aidan didn't let on. Instead, he joked, "The one world where muggles win over the purebloods, huh?"

A Harry Potter reference. *This guy is Mr. Perfect.* "Yes. Just call me Hermione from now on."

"I still prefer Madeleine." Aidan leaned closer and removed her shades from her nose. "I understand more than you know. I'm well aware of the privileges I enjoy for the accident of my birth to an Italian mother and an Irish father. All the Ryan children are. We don't take them for granted." He tucked a wayward curl behind her ear. "I'm sure it wasn't easy street the whole way. You've also had struggles."

Maddie swallowed past the lump in her throat. Aidan could be so tender when he chose to. "There were plenty. Envy and jealousy were always present. From both full Filipinos and mixed. Every casting was questioned—I was too dark for the cosmetic ad, too tall for the shoe brand, too thin to endorse a fast food store. My name change was controversial, as you can imagine." She rolled her eyes at that bit of stupidity.

"The worst was that commercial that made my career. Some girls started a rumor that I slept with the actor to get the role. I was only fifteen. He was early thirties. I looked older than my age, already reached my full height, but still. Eww."

The memory made her shudder with distaste. She took a couple of water bottles out of her bag—one to wash away the bad taste in her mouth, the other for Aidan, whose full attention was focused on her, his lips tight with ... was that anger?

"Who protected you? You were a minor with a guardian who was deathly ill. Who kept away the bad guys?"

"Before the doctors found the malignant lump in her breast, my mom worked as a personal assistant to an entertainment lawyer. Ma asked Andie to draw up airtight contracts that ensured I wasn't exploited or cheated. It helped that my first job was for an all-female advertising agency where Andie's partner, Chris, was the senior creative director." The thought of the couple had Maddie grinning widely. "My fairy godmothers; *they* protected me until I could fend for myself." They'd moved to the US after her graduation, but they'd kept in touch through social media.

"Then your father came and provided you with financial security."

Something about Aidan's words made her stiffen. "My father showed up when I was most vulnerable, and I appreciate all that he's given me, but I like to think that I would have eventually made it on my own without him. Not as comfortable, I admit, but I'd have survived."

Aidan held her face between his hands. His eyes were more silver than blue in their intensity. "I don't doubt it for a second. You'd have more than survived. You'd have thrived."

Maddie melted, turning into a puddle at his feet. People would think the heat caused it. But, no, it was this guy. His words, his actions, they disarmed her. Love, unmistakable and undeniable, burst through her. "Aidan, it means a lot to me to hear you say that. I—"

"*Ahem.*"

The loud clearing of a throat had all the subtlety of thunder. She resented the intrusion into their intimate moment, making her look at the source of the sound with indignation. Her frown was met by the intimidating stare of an authoritative figure.

This would be Aidan a decade from now: silver-haired, commanding, badass.

Aidan recovered first, getting to his feet before helping her to stand. She took the subtle squeeze he gave her hand as a request to let him take the lead, and she pressed in return to indicate her assent. He obviously knew this scary guy.

Any talks of feelings had to be postponed until she and Aidan were in a more conducive environment.

***

"General MacCormack. Mrs. MacCormack. It's a pleasure to see you both again. May I introduce my girlfriend, Madeleine Duvall?" Aidan addressed the striking pair. He was a burly Scot, black-haired, dark-eyed. She was statuesque, dark-skinned, dark-eyed. A Washington power couple.

Lieutenant General Wayne Effing MacCormack on the beach; if he wasn't seeing it with his own eyes, Aidan wouldn't have believed that the Director of the US Defense Intelligence Agency wore anything other than his well-pressed uniforms. Yet, here he was in a short-sleeved plaid shirt, dark jeans, and cowboy boots. Very Texan. Was this a disguise? If so, it wasn't effective. No casual clothes could hide the military bearing and innate arrogance of a man used to giving orders and having them followed with no questions asked.

The three-star general had informed the Defense Attaché Office on Friday that he and his wife were in the country. He had not requested local assistance—he'd indicated it was a personal trip, not an official visit.

However, the coded message Aidan had received this morning said otherwise. He was to suggest a suitable place for a meeting at eleven hundred hours. Once he replied with this location, he'd been ordered to take Madeleine along.

"It's always wonderful to see a familiar face in a foreign country, Aidan," said Mrs. MacCormack, clasping his hand. "And, to finally meet a special someone in your life." The elegant lady smiled warmly at his girlfriend. "Madeleine, a lovely name for a beautiful young woman. We are pleased to meet you. Aren't we, Mac?"

"We certainly are, Ms. Duvall." The general held out his hand and stared pointedly at Madeleine's, still enveloped in Aidan's. He was reluctant to let go.

Ever the poised public relations expert, Madeleine extricated her hand smoothly to accept the customary greeting. "General, Mrs. MacCormack, it's an honor to make your acquaintance. We …" she turned to Aidan with raised brows, then back to the older couple, "… are having a little picnic. Would you like to join us?"

They were? Aidan's lips twitched. He didn't know what else Madeleine had in her magic bag, but in his opinion, a couple of bottled waters didn't make a picnic.

"All the missuses and ranks are too formal, don't you think? Please call me Trisha. I'd like to call you Madeleine."

"Trisha, my friends call me Maddie."

"Maddie, how delightful. Thank you for the invitation." With a smile, Trisha sank gracefully onto the makeshift blanket, followed by Madeleine. "I admit I could use the rest. Mac dragged me to the top of the lookout tower, and I'm tired. The old knees can't take those kinds of climbs anymore."

So, that was how the general had spotted them, probably from the moment they'd crossed the bridge. The old pilot still had eagle eyes.

"Aidan, will you walk with me?"

Pleasantries over. Time for business. "Excuse us, ladies."

They strolled along the beach in silence for a few minutes before the general spoke. "I assume you've taken the necessary steps to ensure you're not running afoul of UCMJ." He referred to the Uniform Code of Military Justice, specifically the cohabitation rules.

"Our living together is not wrongful. We're both single, and Madeleine is not claiming any military benefits," he rattled off. He'd prepared for this.

"Many would say living rent-free at a US government property *is* a benefit."

Playing the devil's advocate, huh. Okay. "It's the same rent whether I'm alone or with a roommate, and the chief of mission gave his approval."

"Ms. Duvall is your beneficiary on your life insurance."

A reminder that Big Brother was always watching. Aidan had purchased the twenty-year-term policy from a local agent the week after his return from Thailand. It was issued only yesterday. "The personal one, yes. Not the group insurance." With half a million dollars, Maddie could set up a business if she wanted to stop working for other people. He hadn't told her yet, and he didn't plan to tell her. If she knew about it, that meant he'd died.

"She's your emergency contact. You gave her the power of attorney on your health directives," his boss persisted.

Surely, this was an exhibition of common sense, not a reason to be shamed. "Madeleine is here in Singapore. My brothers, although nearby, are in other countries. I want someone personally close to me to carry out my wishes instead of an organization that will follow standard operating procedures." He could only hope Madeleine were in town if an accident befell him.

Aidan braced himself for more questions, but the general fell silent once more. When a young couple crossed their path, he understood the lack of conversation. Only when they reached the end of the islet and ensured there was no one around did the older man speak again.

"The task force has completed their analysis on the intel you provided from your last mission in Morocco. They connected it with several other reports from various sources and have identified one of the diplomatic spies suspected of selling top secret information to anti-US factions in Asia, Africa, and Europe for the past decade. The spy in question belongs to a group that wants to put France at the helm of the European Union. And for the EU to be the world's biggest superpower, not Russia, China, or the US."

France? Aidan reeled, suddenly unbalanced. The sand shifted beneath his feet with the oncoming tide. His pulse accelerated. Dread, that slimy creature, slunk into his chest. France had led the creation of the

EU in the late nineties, to check the United States' power in global affairs. They'd gone against the US on several occasions, like the invasion of Iraq in 2003. Even more so lately on various issues from global warming to ISIS.

The French were considered allies; they had access to US information during joint exercises. Aidan had ruled out military. "The spy is a political officer."

"He is the incoming political counselor on strategic and security issues at the *Ministère des Affaires Etrangères Français* in DC. Before his assignment starts, he's going to visit his daughter here in Singapore." General MacCormack dropped the bombshell casually. "I think you know who I'm talking about."

"Jean-Marc Duvall, Madeleine's father." Aidan had disliked the man from the start. He despised him more now that he knew the Frenchman was a traitor, an enemy of the US.

The most important woman in his life was the daughter of his enemy. A daughter who loved her papa, who preferred her once-a-year father to her absentee mother.

What a fucking nightmare.

"Your girlfriend's background check, particularly the financial report and travel list, triggered several red flags. Her name is connected to an untouched numbered Swiss bank account worth more than eleven million euros. It was opened twelve years ago, when she and her father applied for French citizenship by descent. Deposits were made annually, each spring when Ms. Duvall visited her father. Mr.

Duvall hasn't nearly as much money in his account. Only what's reasonable, based on his salary and investments."

Aidan's gaze flew towards Madeleine in the distance. A knot formed in his belly. Eleven million euros? She would laugh at his five-hundred-thousand-dollar death benefit. Was he the next target?

No. Impossible. He shook his head and turned to look at the water while he mulled over the damning information. Eleven million pesos was more believable and more consistent with her declaration on the forms. If Madeleine knew she had millions of euros, she would stay in the Philippines where she was comfortable and where all her friends resided. She wouldn't be busting her ass to find more clients, like Patrick, to add to her already large portfolio.

Aidan kicked at the fine sand as he gave himself a mental thwack in the head for doubting Madeleine, even for one second. Her father wasn't assigned to Singapore. She'd gotten her promotion here before she met him and couldn't have known he was going to Boracay the same time she did. He had been the one who'd arrived at her doorstep in Makati to initiate their weekend fling. The one who had visited her office to re-start their affair. True, she'd agreed quickly to living with him, but it had been he who'd asked.

Confident with his conclusions, Aidan turned back to his boss. "Circumstantial. Madeleine is innocent," he said, defiantly.

"You'd better hope that's true. Currently, you're on track for a two-year below-the-promotion-

SINGAPORE FLING

zone to colonel. This association with the daughter of a spy, an enemy of the US, has the potential to derail your career, or even end it." The general's words held a touch of impatience.

Aidan's hands fisted at his sides. Not too long ago, he'd been a hero for saving his commander's life. Now, he was potentially facing a dishonorable discharge. What the actual fuck? "With all due respect, sir, my record of serving my country speaks for itself. There is no reason to doubt me now. If there are any doubts about that, they just have to look."

"I was planning to take you off the case due to conflict of interest, but this has been your mission from the start of your assignment here. And, because of your relationship with Ms. Duvall, you are best positioned to learn their plans when he comes for a visit. It is clear that the sale of information takes place whenever father and daughter are in the same place. Duvall doesn't get paid unless she shows up, that's why he's coming here. If your girlfriend is only the cover, then she's in the clear. If not, she'll be an accessory to her father's crimes and will be charged accordingly."

He looked his superior officer in the eye. "I will prove Maddie's innocence, as well as ensure Duvall is brought to justice," he promised through gritted teeth.

General MacCormack nodded. "You'll take the lead until it is time for the arrest. The full briefing will be on your desk tomorrow. For your eyes only. We'll have more time to strategize when you accompany me to Hawaii on Tuesday."

After a few yards, the general spoke again. "I trust your instincts, Aidan. It took you only five months to crack the case when others took years without success. You will do the right thing."

"Thank you, sir. I appreciate that." A lightness came into his being after that endorsement, and Aidan relaxed.

He was able to assume a normal front by the time they returned to the spot where the two women were bonding. He even flashed a smile when Madeleine handed him another bottled water and a tube of sunblock.

How heavy was that bag? She'd brought six water bottles, including the ones she gave to the older couple, the sarong, a towel, maybe a change of clothes in case they swam, and possibly a book or an e-reader, and whatever she'd prepared for their picnic. Had he known it had so much stuff in it, he'd have offered to carry it, no matter that it looked feminine with its bright yellow woven straw design. Madeleine's supermodel body hid impressive strength.

"Mac, Maddie gave me some excellent suggestions on where to find the best food."

Food recommendations from Miss Salad-Four-Days-A-Week? Was it chicken rice and more chicken rice? Aidan covered up his laugh with a pretend cough. His loud throat-clearing earned him a glare from his girlfriend. "Sorry, the water went down the wrong way."

"We can go to the hawker centers tomorrow, but for dinner tonight, she suggested this fine-dining place that serves the best chili crab," Trisha continued, naming a Michelin-starred restaurant at Marina Bay that had a six-month-long waiting list.

Probably Madeleine's client, if she could get a table for the MacCormacks with only a few hours' notice.

"Why don't the two of you join us?" Trisha asked Aidan, her face beaming. "I've really enjoyed our chat and would love to know more about Maddie and how you met."

Oh, joy. More interrogation. He shifted his attention to Madeleine for an indication on how she felt about spending more time with the older couple. He received an enthusiastic nod. Okay, then. "If Madeleine is sure we can get a table for four, then we'd love to join you."

He needed the distraction. The document that would arrive on his desk tomorrow might alter the course of his life, and that of Madeleine's. Tonight, he would enjoy the company of friends and the woman who had become the most important woman in his life. Perhaps one who could make or break his career.

If he couldn't prove her innocence, he would lose both her and his job.

He meant to keep both.

CHAPTER FOURTEEN

Aiyoh [Eye yo], interjection – In Cantonese: equivalent to "Oh dear."

"Wait, wait, wait. Back up a bit. Let me get everything straight." Maddie held up a hand to stem the flow of her best friend's excited chatter, then placed the tablet sideways on the coffee table for better viewing. Krista's early video call on Thursday night instead of their usual Saturday afternoon chat was unusual and obviously important. "You and Blake are changing the venue of the wedding from Boracay to Palawan, you're going to resign from the company, and Blake, the CEO, could soon follow. *Oh là là!* You really know how to *carpe diem, m'amie.* I want to be you when I grow up."

Krista burst out laughing. "Yes. Blake and his Perlas partners decided to expand, not only in Palawan, but also in Cebu, Bohol, and somewhere in the north—maybe La Union. They need a full-time management team and offered me the CFO position. Naturally, I accepted. Paraiso will hopefully be finished by the end of November, and since ours is a Christmas wedding, we thought it's fitting to have it on Isla Pasko."

Maddie slapped her forehead. "Duh! Of course. *Pasko is* Christmas. I should have thought of that myself. I'll update the wedding board right away." With its sugar-fine white sand and clear blue waters, the island was perfect for destination weddings. Maddie hadn't been there yet, but the photos Krista had attached to an e-mail showed the spectacular natural beauty of the yet-undeveloped island. "So, the wedding is sort of a soft opening?"

"*Korek*. Official launch is New Year's Day. We want to make sure everything works—the booking system, sea plane operations, food, electricity, Wi-Fi, etcetera. Blake is supposed to brief you about it, but I couldn't wait to share my news with you, so I preempted him." Krista stuck her tongue out, making fun of her own cheekiness.

"As you should. Need I remind you that not only am I your best friend, I'm also your wedding planner and maid of honor?" Maddie declared with a single eyebrow raised.

"Oh, Maddie, you're doing so much for me. I don't know how to thank you."

"Shush. I haven't done anything yet. And if it gets too much, I know how to delegate to *M'amie*," she said. "That's why I called. We're supposed to meet to detail your wedding plans, but I can't go to the Philippines during Holy Week. My father is coming here to visit me around that time." He'd e-mailed to say he'd arrive the last week of March, early April, which was two weeks from today. "Would you and Blake consider visiting me here instead? You haven't met Papa because he never went to Manila, and you always refused to go with me when I traveled to his posts."

"Maddie, you gave me so much when we were in college. You still do to this day. I'm staying at your place rent-free, for heaven's sake. I feel like I'm taking advantage of your generosity. But, those trips were the only times you saw your papa. I couldn't intrude," Krista explained. "I'll have to ask Blake, but I'd love to come. I miss you. It's been three months. We've never gone longer than two weeks without seeing each other."

"Aww. I miss you too, Krissy. Tell Blake he can stay with Aidan in Tanglin while you and I stay at my East Coast flat."

"Why can't we all stay at Aidan's apartment? Isn't it closer to all the sights? Are you two okay? Where did he go this time?" The concern on Krista's face matched her barrage of questions: quick and intense.

"Nothing's wrong. We're great. You sounded like Ange just now. You've been spending too much time with her," Maddie teased. Her friends' closeness didn't bother her too much now that her relationship with Aidan had grown deeper. She wasn't alone anymore. "Think of your temporary separation from Blake as fasting and abstinence, your Lenten sacrifice."

That earned another laugh from her friend.

"We have lots to catch up on, and we can't do that if we're with our boyfriends. Also, the guest room here is the size of my closet." It *was* her closet. "We'll be cramped. The Ryan brothers are not the smallest of men, and neither are we," she pointed to Krista and herself, "the most petite of women." Both of mixed-race origins, at five feet, eight inches they were taller than the average Filipino male, who was usually five feet, three inches in height.

"You look awesome. Even more gorgeous than when you were size zero. You're liking the Singaporean food?"

"I do. In addition to chicken rice and *kaya* toast, I've come to love *sambal* stingray and *bak kut teh*," she confirmed, naming the barbecued fish topped with spice paste and a warming, clear, pork soup that was a perfect rainy-day meal.

Those, however, were not her secret craving. That honor belonged to the scrumptious, highly addictive Salted Egg Fish Skins that her assistant, Rini, had introduced her to. The pleasantly plump older woman had been taking her elder-sister role seriously, making it her mission to put more curves on Maddie's slim frame.

She had to admit, the new figure suited her. She'd never felt sexier than she did now. Aidan had been vocal in his appreciation as well.

Speaking of whom ... "Aidan flew his boss to Hawaii for some Pacific Command meeting on Tuesday. I don't ask details about his job. A lot of it is top secret. I only know what he's willing to reveal."

It was fine with her. She didn't need all the details. While the men had walked and talked on the beach, she'd asked Trisha MacCormack for advice on how to support Aidan in his military career. If their relationship was going to go the distance, she wanted to learn how to cope with incidences like his near air collision in Thailand. The older woman had told her to recognize that danger was part of Aidan's job and that it would be okay for Maddie to worry, but she shouldn't make a fuss. She was trying on that attitude now. "He should be home tomorrow."

Krista's brows pulled together. "Is there anything you want to tell me?"

Maddie exhaled a deep sigh. She couldn't hide anything from her best friend. "I haven't told my father about Aidan yet," she admitted.

"Why not? Your boyfriend is a distinguished military officer, not a bum who's sponging off you. Aren't you proud of him?" Krista's tone was sharp, defensive of her future brother-in-law.

Krista had cause to feel close to Aidan, as they shared the same birthday. They'd celebrated together in Boracay last year. The visit to New York had further strengthened their ties. When Maddie had told Krista about moving in with Aidan, her best friend had been ecstatic for her. Team Maidan, she'd claimed.

"I am. Very much so. That's not the reason for my reluctance. My relationships are not something I discuss with my father. I don't volunteer information. He has asked before, and I'd say if I was involved or not. He never probed any further, but he always extolled the virtues of Frenchmen."

"None of your previous relationships mattered enough to progress to the meet-the-parents stage. This is different, isn't it? Aidan matters. You're falling in love with him." Just like that, Krista gave words to the truth Maddie had been keeping to herself since the night Aidan had given her a massage.

"I already am," she said simply. And she thought Aidan cared for her as well. He'd introduced her as his girlfriend to his boss. It was the sign she'd been waiting for. She'd barely resisted the urge to kiss him right there and then. But they hadn't had the chance to talk about their relationship. Not on Sunday when they returned from dinner. Aidan had been quiet after his conversation with his boss. On Monday, between her upcoming pitch to a prospective client and his preparations for the trip to Hawaii, they'd been too exhausted to do more than kiss each other goodnight.

Krista nodded in understanding. "That's why you won't be able to hide him. Just like I was unable to hide Blake from my *nanay*. You can't, anyway. Aidan is too huge, too important."

"Yes. And too American." Maddie blurted the real reason she hadn't told her papa about Aidan. "My father hates them. Something to do with family history dating all the way back to the Louisiana Purchase. Why he doesn't blame Napoléon is beyond me." She had never attempted to know exactly why. It hadn't affected her life at all. Whatever had happened in the nineteenth century had no bearing at all on the twenty-first.

"I didn't consider my father's antipathy towards Americans when I decided to engage in a relationship with Aidan. It hadn't even occurred to me to factor him in. I am thirty years old, have total control of my life. My father has no say in who I date," she declared. Her vehemence sounded defensive, even to her own ears. And yet, she still wanted her papa to accept her choice, if not approve of it.

"I understand. Been there, done that," Krista said. "What is it you're afraid will happen when they meet?"

"That I may lose one of them. That I may have to choose." She fought the urge to cry.

"Oh, Maddie." Krista went speechless for a few seconds, allowing Maddie to regain her composure. "That's quite the dilemma. Why do you think you'll have to choose?"

"All my life I've been surrounded by women: Ma, Irene, Andie and Chris, you and *M'amie*. My father has been the only constant male presence for almost thirteen years. Aidan changed all that when I agreed to live with him." A little over eight weeks. That was all it took for him to be her person.

"Is there really no chance they'll get along for your sake?"

"No. I'm one hundred percent sure they will clash. Aidan already claimed he could take on my father if they were to fight. That was his first thought. Whatever he knows about Jean-Marc Duvall doesn't impress him, even though I've stressed how Papa came to my aid when Ma was dying." The truth was, Aidan seemed to have a distaste for both her birth parents, which was probably her fault. He'd based his opinion on what she'd told him.

"I don't want to lose my father, Kris. He's been nothing but generous to me. Even though we're not as close as you and your fathers are, he's still the only blood relative I have who seems to want me in his life." Maddie brought her legs up close to her chest. "But, losing Aidan will ... break me," she said, her voice cracking on the last two words. "I've waited so long to finally fall in love, and I don't think I'll ever find another who'll make me feel the same."

"Oh, Mads. I don't know what to say. I'll definitely come now even without Blake. I want to be there for you, whether what you fear happens or not. You can count on me."

"Thanks, Krissy. I really appreciate that." Maddie wiped away the tears.

"You are family, the sister of my heart. I wish we weren't so far away from each other. I want to give you a hug right now."

Maddie opened her arms wide. "Consider it received and returned, *ma sœur*."

"Hey, where's *my* hug?" Blake—wet hair slicked back, towel draped over one naked shoulder—appeared on the screen behind Krista, cutting off their dramafest.

He'd just come in from the pool. When Maddie lived in the same building, she used to swim with Blake, their common choice of exercise. Not so with Aidan, who never took his shirt off in public. Part of his policy was never to have his back exposed. With his preferred exercise regimen of running and yoga, he did not need to go shirtless. The privilege of seeing his wonderfully lean body in its naked entirety was solely hers. *Lucky me.*

"Later, greedy guy," his amused girlfriend admonished, belying her words by wrapping her arms about his waist, unmindful of his damp shorts. Blake responded in kind, bending to press a kiss on the top of her head.

"Gag! You two are too much. I get a toothache from seeing you together," Maddie teased, her tone cheery despite the pang of envy at the sweet display.

She and Aidan weren't there yet. The most they'd done in public to establish their couplehood was to hold hands in front of the general and his wife. They expressed their intimacy best behind closed doors. In the bedroom, they couldn't keep their hands off each other.

"Hello, Maddie. I'm sure Krista gave you the news already." Blake addressed her with a knowing look on his face. He reached down to tickle his fiancée's neck, sending her into a fit of giggles.

"Of course she did. Congratulations! So, you're going to be a full-time hotelier, huh?"

"In a couple of months, yes. It's a gamble, but what the heck. *Carpe diem*. Right, love?"

"Seize the day!" her formerly uber-cautious best friend cheered, raising her arm in the air as if it were a battle cry. She twisted around to plant a kiss on her fiancé's cheek.

"Hey, whatever love potion you're both drinking, can we mass-produce it and sell it at your resorts? The profits will be so humongous, you can buy another island." She meant to say it in jest, but it came out with a bite.

The smiles on Blake's and Krista's faces fell. "Maddie!" Krista's censure came swiftly.

"I'm sorry. It came out wrong. Don't mind me. I'm tired. It's almost ten. I have to go to bed." And sulk that she and Aidan didn't get to talk today. He'd called, but she'd missed it. Eighteen hours difference sucked.

"You sleep at ten now?"

Krista was *this* close to losing her best friend status. "Yes. You didn't have to sound so incredulous.

I wake up at six to be early for work. And before you ask, yes, it's really me. I've changed. It was my New Year's resolution. I've been sticking to it so far." No way would she be accused of tardiness ever again. Not by her Singaporean colleagues, and definitely not by Aidan.

"Don't let us keep you from your beauty rest, then. Give my brother a hug when he returns. I'm assuming he's gone, that's why you're alone."

"Yes, he's in Hawaii for work."

"Yeah, the Air Force's idea of work in an island paradise and mine are worlds apart. I prefer mine, but theirs is necessary." Respect for his brother's work rang true in Blake's voice.

"Don't sell yourself short, honey. Your jobs, both present and future, benefit thousands of people." Krista's support of her future husband was absolute.

Aiyoh! This cooing could go on for a while. "Guys, you're both right. Kris, I changed my mind. I want the two of you to stay at my place on the East Coast. I'll see you soon." Maddie clicked the screen off without waiting for the two's response and slumped back on her seat.

She loved Krista and Blake. She was happy for them. But seeing them together reminded her of what she wanted but didn't have. Yet.

Maybe Krista and Blake had it right, *carpe diem*-ing their decisions in life. There were no guarantees for their future. Today was the only day that mattered.

If she told Aidan she loved him, what was the worst thing that could happen? That he didn't love her back. But, what if he did?

Aargh! She was going to give herself a headache with these thoughts, and that would make sleep difficult. She did need to be early at work in the morning, as she was leading a pitch. If tomorrow came, she'd seize the day. For now, it was time to hit her lonely bed.

CHAPTER FIFTEEN

Kiasu [kyä so͞o], adj. – In Hokkien: afraid to lose; overly competitive.

Aidan frowned down at the tablet Madeleine had left on the coffee table. She'd gone to the balcony to take a work call, grumbling under her breath at the discourtesy of clients calling on a Saturday morning. The tablet lay open on a Notes page.

>Kalanggaman, Leyte
>Calaguas, Camarines Norte
>Maira-Ira, Ilocos Norte
>Tablas, Romblon
>Matukad, Caramoan.

A list of islands in the Philippines and the provinces where they were located. Under all the names were two words: twelve million.

Bile churned in Aidan's gut. Twelve million dollars or euros? If the pattern continued, one million euros were due to be deposited into Madeleine's Swiss bank account in two weeks, giving her twelve, plus whatever interest it had gained over the years. Had she known all along about her father's illegal activities? He'd assured the general she knew nothing about the money. Did she make him a liar?

In Hawaii, he'd managed to verify Madeleine's financial report from a secured computer, and everything had checked out. He'd looked up every combination of Madeleine "Maddie" Estrella Duvall. Except for the condo and the Porsche, she had no other extravagant expenses that were not accounted for by her salary and bonuses. None of her Philippine bank accounts showed irregular transactions or massive transfers within the last five years.

With regard to the Swiss account in her name, his investigation had concluded that she hadn't made the deposits from her native country. It still didn't clear her—that would only have happened if they'd been able to trace the sources of the transfers and none of them was Madeleine. On Wednesday, the defense attaché office sent an official request to the bank in Geneva through the US Embassy for complete cooperation, but as of Friday, they hadn't received a response.

A deeper dive into her social media activities for the past dozen years showed little of her association with her father. Most of her photos from her visits to Jean-Marc Duvall's assignments consisted of solos in front of popular tourist spots. None were of father and daughter together.

While Aidan hated having something in common with the bastard, this he understood. Except for official purposes or family portraits—which his mother insisted upon after every major milestone—he never posed for pictures. Men who worked in the shadows like Jean-Marc Duvall and himself couldn't afford the exposure.

"Snooping, Colonel Ryan?" Madeleine's voice behind him held a snap to it.

The waspish tone ignited his temper, making his turn more abrupt than he'd intended. She stood beside the sofa with her arms crossed, eyes flashing, even white teeth bared in a snarl.

"Hardly. I didn't touch anything. Why? Do you have something to hide?"

"You mean to tell me the almighty United States Intelligence hasn't found out my deepest, darkest secrets yet? It's been ten days since my interview. *Tsk, tsk, tsk*. Slow much?"

Shit. She couldn't know how close she was to the truth. He couldn't tell her anything without revealing his mission. The US government needed to confront Jean-Marc here in Singapore, where he did not have diplomatic immunity. Once he started work in DC, he would be virtually untouchable. Aidan couldn't risk the possibility that she'd warn her father away from their meeting.

Folding his tall frame onto the low cushioned seat, he evaded the question, choosing instead to douse the fire that was his girlfriend's temper. "Why are you taking swipes at me? I'd appreciate it if you sheathe your claws. I'm not fighting with you."

Her forehead furrowed, Madeleine stared at him without blinking for a few seconds before she exhaled an audible huff of breath. He took it to mean she'd decided to give up the belligerence. She dropped her phone on the table with a thud and plopped down beside him gracelessly. "I lost a pitch, okay? The potential client went with a boutique agency because they want," she raised her hands to do air quotes, "personalized service."

She kicked off her slippers with such force, they flew over the coffee table in front of them. "They just want to be cheap; that's why they're going with the small company instead of mine."

"And you're taking it out on me because …"

"Because you have the misfortune of being here. Surely, you don't expect me to be all sweetness and light all the time. I'm not the kind of woman who bottles things up inside. I let it out. Would you rather I scream and bring the attention of the Marines to our unit?"

"Of course not. We're already on their watch list because of your fire alarm abuse."

That earned him a ferocious scowl. "They're super sensitive. A whiff of smoke, and they blare instantly," Madeleine groused.

Aidan fought the urge to laugh. "I bought you a new toaster. Yet you still manage to burn bread."

"Only the first time I used it, and you never let me live it down," she said, glowering at him. "I know what you're doing, you know."

"What? Distracting you to stop you from being crabby? It's working, isn't it? See, you're smiling now." He turned her around and rubbed the tightness between her shoulders that he knew was always there. "I'm sorry you didn't get the business. I'm sure you gave it your best."

With her head bowed, Madeleine leaned back into his touch, grunting in pain when he pressed hard on a particularly tight knot at the base of her neck. "Thank you. I'm sorry for taking it out on you. I hate losing."

Aidan chuckled at the grumpy admission. "I noticed that about you. That's why I won't ever play poker with you again. You cheat."

"Ha! I told you to ask Blake how to play *pusoy dos*, but you couldn't be bothered. You keep insisting you know how to play poker, which is different. That's why you lose." She dropped her head on the crook of his neck, well-relaxed now, good humor restored. "Thanks, Aid," she said a couple of breaths later.

Aid. He stilled. That was the first time she called him by a nickname. To his ear, it sounded like an endearment. Something moved within his chest. He'd been keeping her at arm's length by calling her Madeleine. It was time he stopped.

"You're welcome, Maddie." He settled her more comfortably between his legs, his arms encircling her waist. "So, what's the list about? Are you buying an island or five?" He had to ask even if only to ease his mind.

Maddie twisted around to poke his chest. "Aha! You *were* snooping."

"If I was snooping, I wouldn't have to ask you questions. I'd already know the answer."

"How did you know I'm looking up islands then?"

"The tablet was on the most recent app you opened. It turned on when I placed my mug beside it. You should always secure it with a password."

"Why bother? It's my personal one. I only use it to read e-books, play the occasional game, and video chat with *M'amie*."

"You don't know how much your online footprint can reveal about you to cyber criminals. It's a surprise to me you haven't been hacked yet. Anyway, islands? Twelve million dollars. Are you buying?" Even if she only received a percentage of the entire Swiss bank account, it would still be enough to purchase an island in this region.

"I wish. That's my dream, you know. My own island. Maybe someday," she said, eyes warm with wistfulness. "And that's twelve million pesos. Less than a quarter of a million dollars, the cheapest I could find. It's not for me."

Pesos. Aidan breathed a sigh. A rare time he was glad to have been wrong. "I thought you didn't bring work home. That's why you stay late at the office some days."

"I don't normally, but this is for Krista and Blake."

"Isn't their wedding happening in Boracay? Why are you looking at other locations for them? Are they buying an island?" He knew his brother was well-off, but to have a quarter of a million ready at a moment's notice boggled his mind. He, himself, was only worth half a million dollars. It had taken him years of frugal living and prudent investments to accumulate that. Serving in the military didn't make one rich; that was why many were vulnerable to bribes, like those involved in the Big Ken scandal here in Singapore a few years ago.

"Krista told me the other night that they're changing the venue to Palawan. They're also expanding the business to other islands in the country.

SINGAPORE FLING

You came in too late last night for me to tell you. I guess Blake hasn't informed the family yet. I'll have to make sure everyone is updated. Here's where you can help as best man."

"I'm due for a check-in with Ma and Da tonight. I'll let them know," he promised. Taking the opportunity, he said in the most neutral tone he could manage, "Speaking of parents, when are yours coming?"

Maddie's brows knotted. "Papa? At the end of the month. The last time I spoke with Irene regarding her latest address, she didn't say anything about visiting," she said with a careless shrug and raised chin.

Noticing the pain caused by her mother's neglect, Aidan reached out a hand to stroke Maddie's arms. "Tell me what happens when you meet with your father," he said. To distract and, despite the twinge in his conscience, to gather information. The more he knew, the better his chances of proving her innocence.

Maddie shifted to sit across from him and arranged her legs in a lotus pose before answering. "I'm expecting it'll be different this time because he's the one visiting me. Usually, if it's somewhere I haven't been, I'd stay for over a week. Arrive Saturday, leave the next. Papa would take me sightseeing on Sunday and we'd have dinner every night, sometimes with the current wife, many times just the two of us. I'd stay in a hotel chain—my client's if they have one in that city."

That caught his attention. "You never stayed with your father?"

"No. He said his residences are often bugged." Madeleine paused, widened her eyes, then leaned forward to whisper, "Is this place clean?"

Aidan nodded. "The US has a long-term lease here, and we check regularly for surveillance." With Russian and Chinese embassies in the same area, they had to stay vigilant. As for Duvall's claim, it was a valid excuse, and it was convenient for his treachery. He could leave a portable drive somewhere in Maddie's room for somebody else to retrieve later. Once the top secret information was secured, the money transfer would automatically follow. "Since the situation is reversed, will he be the one to stay in a hotel, or will you invite him to your East Coast apartment?"

"Hotel, for sure. I already promised the flat to Krista and Blake. Because of the change of venue and there being only nine months to go, the three of us need to have some serious wedding-planning time."

Aidan chewed on the information for a bit, weighing its implications while Maddie enumerated the agenda of her future discussions with the engaged couple. Since he expected things to go south with Maddie and her father, he figured his girlfriend would need her best friend's support while he completed his mission. A challenge, however, would be accessing Duvall's hotel room. The man surely knew how to detect bugs and prepare a trip alarm. The best scenario would be to lure him to a location that Aidan's team could control.

Unfortunately, that lure came in the form of Madeleine.

Aidan's chest tightened. He preferred not to use her as bait, but it was inevitable.

His and General MacCormack's brainstorming this past week in Hawaii kept circling back to that plan. Aidan intended to find another way, and he hoped to accomplish that before his first meeting with the task force next week. To apprehend Jean-Marc Duvall, they needed a representative from the Federal Bureau of Investigation, the French embassy, and the Singapore government. They'd set up what they could until Madeleine heard from her father about his exact itinerary.

"I'll tell Blake you agreed to wear a *barong* for the wedding." Maddie broke into his thoughts with the incomprehensible statement.

"I'm sorry, I wasn't listening," She'd said something about a *barong.* He didn't mind wearing the formal Filipino shirt at all. Loose and thin, it was more appropriate for a wedding in the Philippines than a suit anyway. Especially on a beach.

"I know." Maddie huffed. "Your eyes glazed over the second I mentioned the word 'wedding.'"

That wasn't the reason he'd drifted off, but he would take it. He pulled Maddie onto his lap. "I have no doubt that with your style and my brother's managing ways, he and Krista will have the best wedding ever."

"You said you'll help. That's why we're together." Her lips pulled down into a pout.

"That was just an excuse. We're together because we both want to *be* with each other. Like this."

Aidan held her face between his hands and pressed a soft kiss to her lips. "I like being with you, Maddie."

"I love being with you too, Aid," she said against his mouth before slanting her lips against his and kissing him sweetly.

Love.

He hadn't said it, but it felt right. They felt right.

Together.

He vowed to do everything he could to keep them that way.

CHAPTER SIXTEEN

Arrow [ˈerō], n. – In Singlish: an order being directed at someone, like an arrow, to carry out a task, usually against their wishes.

Aidan paced the confines of the meeting room while he waited on the arrival of his visitors. He couldn't sit still. Soundproofed and fortified, this was the most secure room in the US Embassy. It was equally useful for top secret discussions and a shelter from natural disasters, like earthquakes. A long table sat ten people. Nothing adorned the walls. Cell phones weren't allowed inside. Aidan had always been comfortable in this room until today—the day before he completed his mission. There were aspects of this Friday's operation that he wasn't happy with. All of them involved Maddie.

Two peremptory knocks sounded, and the door opened to admit two men in matching black suits. Aside from their clothing, they were a study in contrast, almost caricatures of their nationalities. The American was basketball-player tall at six feet, nine inches, dark, and rumpled. The Frenchman, a naval officer, was a foot shorter, pale, and dapper.

Aidan held out his hand first to his counterpart, the French Embassy's Defense Cooperation Attaché. "*Capitaine* Michaud, *merci d'être venu.*" After his greeting was returned, he shook hands with the Federal Bureau of Investigation's legal attaché. "Special Agent Harris, thank you for coming."

He gestured to the chairs clustered around the table. "Please," Aidan invited. Once they'd taken their seats, he sat at the head of the table. Tomorrow, he'd relinquish the seat to the legal attaché. For now, this remained his show to run.

"I'm sorry to call you here on such short notice. I have new information to share." He handed both a sheaf of documents.

Agent Harris folded his hands in front of him. "Before I read this, I'd like to reiterate the importance of sticking to the plan we and our respective governments have agreed to. Ms. Duvall is the key to this entire operation, and she will not be excused because of her personal relationship with you."

Aidan wanted to deck the inflexible man. He settled for strangling his pen with his fist. They'd tangled over this subject on many occasions. There was more than enough proof to charge Duvall with espionage, without the need to involve Maddie.

From the intel, Duvall hadn't used his daughter as an unwitting conduit until her second annual visit, but when he had, there'd been deadly consequences. The Defense Intelligence Agency pieced together the timelines of American setbacks in the regions where Duvall was assigned, and they always happened in late spring or early summer.

Because he'd been in Paris, Maddie's father had not acquired any information to sell this time. With his upcoming US assignment, Jean-Marc Duvall didn't need to use Maddie as cover. What he needed was access to funds to enable him to rise to the EU position he had dreamed of achieving. He'd been selling for years. Now, it was time to buy.

"Noted," Aidan gritted out. "But I would like to stress that we owe Madeleine for this opportunity, and that should be taken into consideration when decisions are made regarding her involvement with her father's activities." Had she and her father met in Paris in February, Duvall wouldn't have needed to come to Singapore. He would have conducted the transaction then. Agent Harris wouldn't get credit for the collar.

The French captain coughed to gain attention. "We received Monsieur Duvall's final *itinéraire de voyage*. He's arriving at *seize heures trente-cinc* from Charles de Gaulle, via Air France, and will depart for Geneva aboard British Airways six hours later."

"Duvall is only going to be here from four thirty-five to ten thirty-five? Not even overnight? Fucker is confident he can accomplish his goal that quickly," Agent Harris observed, looking at Aidan pointedly. "Does your girlfriend know this?"

"Madeleine spoke with her father last night." Aidan's jaw muscles ticked at the provocation.

He hadn't been surprised when she'd uninvited him and Krista after the call. "She reserved a private dining room at Saint Michel for eighteen hundred hours," he said. "I already called to reserve it and the one next to it for seventeen hundred."

The FBI legal attaché scribbled on the top paper of the stack Aidan had handed him. "We'll have our people mixed in with the staff. They'll set up listening devices."

This was the trap, simple and basic. Their case depended on Jean-Marc Duvall admitting to anti-American sentiments and claiming ownership of millions of euros in a secret Swiss bank account—things he'd skillfully hidden in his thirty years of foreign service.

Everything hinged on Maddie having no knowledge of the account and questioning her father about it. Plan B was for Aidan to gatecrash the dinner, make the other man angry, and provoke him into showing his true self. Either way, it was going to be messy.

"Colonel Ryan, how sure are you of your girlfriend's innocence?" Agent Harris challenged him once again.

"One hundred percent." Aidan's heart swelled with pride at the same time his conscience pricked with guilt. He pointed to the papers he'd given the two men. "The Swiss bank came through with the trace of the deposits, and they were mainly from three sources. One is based in Dubai, another in the US, and the last in France. Each time, they were made to appear as if wired from a bank in Duvall's location during Madeleine's visits." He waited until the men turned to the next page before speaking again. "Madeleine never visited a local bank. Her practice was to exchange money at the airport and pay with her card as much as possible."

Maddie kept detailed itineraries and expense reports of all her trips among her files. It had been incredibly easy for him to access them. She'd heeded his warning and had passcode-protected her laptop, tablet, and phone. However, she'd also written said code on a sticky note. Finding it would have been a face-palm moment if not for the burst of joy he'd felt when he realized that her code was the day they'd first met—November 2nd of the previous year, his birthday. It was all the proof he needed to confirm that she loved him, though she hadn't told him yet. In exchange, he'd invaded her privacy. He'd felt like an asshole and still did.

"This still doesn't alter the fact that her signature was on the application to open the Swiss account," the agent pointed out.

"Which is easily explained by her lack of fluency in the language when she signed it," Aidan fired back. "She was a teenaged girl who'd been grieving her aunt's death. It doesn't require much imagination to surmise that she could have been overwhelmed by all the paperwork her newfound father presented to her. The Swiss account was submitted as her financial guarantee for the citizenship application, even though it wasn't necessary for the category they applied for. Copies are all there thanks to Captain Michaud and his team."

"It was our pleasure, Colonel Ryan. We appreciate all your work in identifying Monsieur Duvall as a spy. The friendship between our countries is important to us. We will not allow any threats to that friendship go unpunished." He nodded to the agent. "Monsieur Harris, thank you for arranging the extradition quickly. Good luck to us tomorrow." He rose to his feet, to signal the end of the meeting.

Aidan rounded the table to clasp the other man's hand. "*Merci, Capitaine* Michaud. I'll see you tomorrow." To Agent Harris he gave a curt nod.

When they were gone, he returned to his seat and slumped in his chair. He'd done all he could to protect Madeleine. Why did he feel like he'd done nothing at all? She would still be on her own tomorrow to face her father. If Jean-Marc hurt her, there was nothing he could do.

There was no "if" about it: Madeleine's father would break her heart. Aidan could only hope his Maddie would forgive him for his role in that. He feared she would hate him instead. He was afraid she would lose her love for him, that he would lose her. It would be unbearable; he'd never forgive himself.

***

The thud of the door closing behind Krista and Blake and the snick of the latch gave Aidan immense satisfaction. "I thought they'd never leave," he grumbled to Maddie, making her laugh. They'd come home to Tanglin after dinner at the nearby Holland Village to talk some more. He and his brother had discussed Blake's decision to resign from the manufacturing company job to manage his resorts full time, while Maddie and Krista chatted about everyone they knew in the Philippines like they hadn't been video chatting every Saturday afternoon for the past three months. "It's ten pm on a Thursday, and we're going to see them again tomorrow at lunch." He joined her on the couch where she sat with her feet up.

"They're here to see us," she said in a reasonable tone. "I don't know why you're so grumpy. We don't have work tomorrow. Good Friday is a national holiday in Singapore." Maddie nudged his leg with her bare toes. As she had since the first day she'd visited here, she'd left her shoes by the entryway the moment they'd arrived home.

He reached for one foot and massaged her instep, which elicited a throaty moan from her. "I know that. But, they're here until Sunday. I just want you fully rested for tomorrow."

"Why? For the meeting with Papa? It's in the evening. I don't need to sleep early for that."

If she only knew. Aidan wished he could prepare her. Anything he said against her father now would make her suspicious. She wouldn't believe him anyway. In her eyes, Jean-Marc Duvall could do no wrong. He hoped that when Maddie realized she'd been used, she would be able to draw strength from the love of her friends. And him.

Now, all Aidan could do was show her he cared for her. Maybe that would help his case afterwards, when she learned his involvement. "Who said you're sleeping early?"

That got him a raised eyebrow. "I'm not?"

"No. I said rest, not sleep." He gave the other foot equal attention.

"And how am I going to do that?" Maddie wiggled both eyebrows playfully.

"You'll see." Aidan patted both feet before standing. "Follow me to the bathroom in five minutes," he said over his shoulder as he walked to their bedroom.

"Are you going to draw me a bath, Aid?" Maddie called out after him.

Aidan turned to see her on her feet, ignoring his directions. "You are so clever, Maddie-mine. However did you guess?" He was determined to keep this light. Maddie had been happy all evening. She'd been vivacious, her laughter constant and infectious.

Maddie's eyes sparkled. She stuck her tongue out when she drew abreast and hooked her arm around his waist. "Is this your version of washing of the feet?" she asked, referring to the Christian practice of reenacting the humble act by Jesus towards his apostles during the Holy Thursday church service.

"That is a very unsexy and sacrilegious thought, Madeleine Estrella Duvall," Aidan fake-scolded to hide his guilt. Maundy Thursday, the night before the betrayal and death of the savior. How appropriate.

He busied himself with the mechanics of preparing a bubble bath: placing the stopper in, turning the faucet on all the way to the hottest it could go, dropping a bath bomb, pouring liquid soap and oil until the fragrant smells suffused the air. Raising his voice above the roar of the running water, he said, "But if that sort of thing turns you on, then yes, you know I'll take you there."

Maddie, who was unzipping her dress, pealed out a throaty laugh. "Did you just quote Madonna's 'Like a Prayer'? That's so retro."

Delighted with her quick wit, Aidan's lips curved into a smile. "Call me old one more time, and I'll throw you into cold water instead of the boiling inferno you prefer to bathe in," he warned, even as he adjusted the temperature to one that would not result in third degree scalding.

"I didn't say you're old. Actually, thirty-six is the perfect age for a love interest in romance. Not too young. Not ancient, either. I read somewhere you're what they call 'seasoned,'" she said with an accompanying wink.

"Like food? Salted and peppered." Aidan acted offended. "Am I just a piece of meat to you, Maddie?" He undressed and flexed, knowing it amused her when he did it. His cock stirred to semi-erect as her gaze followed his disrobing with heated interest.

Clad only in bra and boy short panties, she sat on the lip of the oval tub, arranging her hair into a bun. Her sensuality was so innate that he was seduced by every move she made. "Hmm." She eyed him up and down, finger on her chin, simulating contemplation. "White meat, perfect with ginger and garlic."

Aidan spluttered. "If you think I'm flattered to be likened to your favorite chicken rice, you're ... not entirely wrong."

She laughed as she removed her underthings.

He stepped into the tub, heart light. "Get your objectifying butt in here, missy," he commanded, spreading his legs and resting them on the porcelain sides. While the scented water was only waist high, the bubbles reached up to his chest, spilling over the two-foot-deep tub. He'd smell like vanilla—like Maddie—but he'd tolerate it for her.

Maddie complied with a grin, sinking gracefully into the warm water. She rested against him, her head tucked under his chin. Body soft and loose in front of him, she breathed a soft sigh.

To his ears, she sounded content. He wrapped his arms around her, glad that he could give this moment to her. She didn't want for material things. Neither did he. Paying attention and taking care of the other by performing various deeds were their love language. He cherished these quiet, intimate moments. With their busy lives, these were rare and special.

They stayed like that until half of the bubbles had popped, the slosh of the water and their even breathing the only sounds in the steamy bathroom.

"Thank you for this, Aid," Maddie said, her voice hushed.

"You're welcome. I need it too." The meeting with his French counterpart and the legal attaché had stressed him. He wanted tomorrow's operation finished so he and Maddie could move on to more important things in their relationship.

"This has been a great day. Krista is here. Dinner was delicious. Oyster omelette, fish head curry, wanton *mee*. Yum!" She leaned to the side and kissed his cheek. "And now, this. Life is good."

"It is, indeed." He dropped a kiss on her shoulder, pleased that she appreciated his efforts.

Maddie gave a little shimmy in the circle of his arms. "Tomorrow is going to be even better. A holiday, and Papa is visiting me for the first time."

Aidan mentally recoiled at the unwelcome reminder. He willed his body not to tense. As close as they were, Maddie would feel his stress. He reached for the bath sponge and stroked her arms and neck to hide his agitation.

"I'm sorry you won't get to meet Papa. He said he didn't have a lot of time, and there's something important he wants to discuss with me alone."

He'd heard everything the previous night. Duvall had called a little after six and told his daughter his flight schedule. Aidan hadn't had to snoop, for Maddie had a habit of turning on the phone speaker.

"It's fine. I'm sure there'll be other opportunities for us to meet in the future," he said. Maddie couldn't know how soon that meeting would be. "Do you have any idea what the 'important thing' is that he wants to discuss?" he asked casually.

Maddie draped her legs over his for him to wash. "None whatsoever. I don't think he's divorcing Vivien and marrying again. Maybe they're going to have a baby." She grinned up at him. "I'd love to have a half-sibling or two. I'll spoil them rotten."

Aidan gripped the sponge so tight, he drained it of moisture. The yearning in Maddie's voice saddened him. There was no upcoming baby. Vivien Duvall was not pregnant. If she was, it wasn't her husband's child. Jean-Marc had a vasectomy when he turned fifty, ten years ago.

A baby. An image of a black-haired, brown-eyed little girl flashed in his mind. She'd have her mother's beauty and his height. Their child. His and Maddie's. Without thinking, his hand dragged the sponge to Maddie's flat stomach. "Do you want to have children?"

She stilled in his arms for a second before resting her head on his shoulder. "Yes. At least one." She exhaled a soft whish of breath against his neck. "But not yet. Before I turn thirty-five for sure," she said in a perkier voice, but he still heard the wistfulness she tried to hide.

Aidan, who'd never planned anything long-term, was all of a sudden dreaming of babies with the woman in his arms. If this wasn't love, he didn't know what else it could be.

But his secrets restricted him from declaring it tonight. While he hadn't outright lied, he'd kept information from Maddie, and that would put his sincerity in question. Honesty was the first rule they'd agreed on, and he'd willfully broken it.

He had to wait until she'd believe him. Tonight would be more about actions than words.

"Four more years, huh." With his toes, Aidan pulled up the stopper to drain the tub. Pressing his mouth to her neck, he whispered, "You'll have a lot of time to practice." The goosebumps he caused to rise on her smooth skin and the ripple of her shiver beneath his hands ignited his primal instincts. "You're going to need a partner who knows what he's doing." *Me. No one else.*

Slickened by the soapy water, Maddie slid around to face him, her bright gaze boring into his. She ran her hands over his shoulders and chest, and breathed, "A seasoned lover. Lean ... tender ... rare ..."

"And now, I'm a steak." With both feet planted on the textured floor, one hand on Maddie's bottom and the other on the edge, Aidan levered them onto the rim.

"Aid, we need to rinse."

He swung his legs over and stood, and she squeaked, clinging to him as much as their slippery bodies allowed.

"Later. Grab a towel if you don't want the sheets to get wet." The second she did, Aidan carried her to their bedroom in a few brisk strides. Her slip-sliding in his arms rubbed him in all the right ways. His cock was primed, ready to pound hard and fast.

But tonight was for giving, not taking. Tonight was for Maddie, not him.

He lowered her to her feet beside their bed and took the towel from her.

"I can dry myself," she protested, but she released the fabric at his tug.

"I know you can. I want to do it for you. Will you let me?" When she sent him a questioning look, he said, "Please?"

Please forgive me for keeping secrets from you.
Please remember tonight.
Please know how much I love you.

Her nod of assent felt like an absolution that he didn't deserve, but that he wanted more than anything else.

Soft pats burst the bubbles that still clung to her silky skin. Gentle swipes dried most of the moisture from her body.

He'd get her wet again, Aidan promised himself as he laid them both down on the bed.

He'd get her hot. It wouldn't take much. It never had.

One kiss. All they needed to set fire to their passion for each other.

As if she'd read his mind, Maddie reached up to twine her arms around his shoulders and pulled him to her. "Kiss me, Aidan," she murmured against his lips.

"Gladly, Maddie."

She asked for kisses. He granted them generously. He sipped at her lips, delved into her sweetness, gave all he could, and took all she offered. He stole her breath when she gasped for it. He left no part of her body wanting attention. Every shiver, every moan, every plea for more sounded like music to his ears.

He worshiped her, scorched himself with her wet heat. He told her of his love with his mouth, his hands, his entire body. When they joined, when she'd found her peak, when he climaxed, he felt complete.

In the quiet aftermath of their lovemaking, he held her close as she slept. Whispered the words he couldn't say.

Maddie-mine, please forgive me.
Don't forget tonight.
I love you.

CHAPTER SEVENTEEN

Jialat [jee ya lat], n. – In Hokkien: a dire situation.

What was it with the men in her life and their inclination to take her out in public only to hide her away in a private dining room? Aidan did it on their first date. Now, Maddie waited for her father to join her at a high-end French restaurant in a hotel overlooking Marina Bay, the country's new downtown. Across the bay was the stunning Sands hotel with its surfboard roof connecting three towers. This side held Merlion, Singapore's most recognizable symbol: a porcelain-plated statue that bore the head of a lion and the body of a fish.

Maddie stared, mesmerized by the bright streetlights, shimmering around the water that spouted from the mythical beast's mouth. Thinking of her country's similar but lesser known sea-lion, called Ultramar, she couldn't help but admire Singapore's branding geniuses for the incredible success of their tourism icon.

"*Mon étoile, tu es plus belle à chaque fois que je te vois.*" The gravelly voice complimenting her looks announced her father's arrival.

"*Ça va*, Papa?" Her face wreathed in smiles to reflect her joy, Maddie stood to greet her papa, accepting and returning the four cheek-kisses that had been their practice since she'd learned how to *faire la bise*. "*Merci*. You're the one who gets better-looking every time I see you."

While it was true, he had also grown visibly older since she'd visited him in London last April. His hair was more gray than dark blond. Both his hair and his physique were thinner. Was he ill? Her eyes narrowed to scrutinize him as they took their seats across from each other. The black briefcase he placed on the floor beside his chair snagged her attention. It seemed incongruous with the informality of this meeting.

"*Parlons français, d'accord?*" Jean-Marc pinned her with an admonishing glare from striking hazel eyes, similar to her own. They'd had to do a DNA test for the citizenship application, but the results only confirmed what they'd known as fact from the first moment they'd met.

This was part of their ritual. "I'll try. But you know it's not my native tongue."

"Madeleine," he intoned, shaking his head. "*Chère enfant*, how long have you been studying *la langue française*? Thirteen years? Why have you not mastered it yet?"

She was considered advanced level, but not yet a Master in her last French fluency test. "You're the only person with whom I speak it." And her boss Pierre, but she wouldn't mention him to her father right now. "I can't break out my French when people are speaking to me in English or Filipino, can I?"

Maddie loved the language. Speaking it, affecting the accent, made her feel superior. A cut above the rest. It gave her a competitive advantage at work. According to Pierre, her French proficiency had given her the winning edge over all the other applicants. She had planned to enroll at the *Alliance Française de Singapour* to improve, but between her job and living with Aidan, she hadn't found time to attend classes.

"Get a French boyfriend," was the response from behind the menu.

"Yeah, about that ..." Maddie trailed off when the manager came in to take their orders. She began again after the white-suited Singaporean left. "I already have a boyfriend. I wanted you to meet him and my best friend, but you said you preferred to see me alone. Is there something wrong?"

Both she and Krista were disappointed with her father's preference. Her friend had wanted to thank Papa for including her in the birthday and Christmas gifts he'd sent to Maddie during college. She wrote a thank-you note instead.

Aidan was weirdly understanding, empathetic even. Before he'd left earlier for some mysterious work on a holiday, he'd told her, "If you need me to be with you while you're meeting your father, call me. I'll be there right away." Then he'd kissed her and hugged her tight for a full minute without letting go. He'd acted reluctant to leave and kept looking at her as if he wanted to say more but decided against it. It had confused her as much as last night's tender lovemaking had given her hope for their future together.

Men: Maddie didn't know what to make of the ones she loved. She'd built up this huge clash in her mind between the two most important men in her life when they eventually met, and for it not to happen unsettled her. It felt like unfinished business, a cliffhanger. She disliked it in books, more so in real life.

"It's nothing bad. I'm just being selfish. Can you forgive your old papa for wanting to keep you to himself?" He reached over the table to hold her hand.

Maddie's lips curved at the charm her father was pouring on. "*Vieux?* Who's old? I'm only eighteen, so you must be thirty-six, right?"

"Thirty-eight, but who's counting?" He squeezed her hand and let go. "Thank you for humoring me. I'd like to hear about them. Maybe after we catch up, *hein*?

"*D'accord.*" Best to have him fed first before she dropped her news about Aidan. "Okay, tell me where I will be visiting you next."

"I'll be assigned to DC," he spat, his facial expression a thundercloud.

"Where? Washington? I thought you detest the US. Didn't you tell me your family got cheated out of their lands in Louisiana?"

Her father placed a finger against his lips, his eyes darting to the room entrance. "*Ssh*, not too loud. And that's *our* family."

Maddie leaned closer to whisper. "If you hate the USA so much, why accept an assignment there?"

He twisted his lips into a contemptuous sneer. "*L'ambition*, what else? I've been promised a plum position in the EU if I take up this post."

Maddie shook her head in bemusement. Thousands of top diplomats dreamed of an assignment in the US. Only her father thought it was a hardship post.

Her father's surliness disappeared when dinner arrived. He had good reason, for the restaurant lived up to high expectations with its mouthwatering French twist on local favorites: spicy canapés of chili crab mousse in *kuih pie tee* shells, savory *laksa* bisque topped with rich lobster *thermidor*, and crispy duck leg confit served over the fruit and vegetable salad that Southeast Asians called *rojak*.

Maddie's papa regaled her with amusing stories about his latest wife Vivien, some of the people he'd met at parties, and visiting politicians he'd had to tour around Paris. His gaiety stopped when he went into a tirade against the current American president.

Aiyayay. This is not going to be easy.

Replete from their dinner, Jean-Marc sat back in his chair, sipping port, exuding bonhomie. "Tell me about this *branleur* you're dating."

"Papa, Aidan's not a wanker. He's a great guy."

"I joke. Tell me more about him."

Describing your lover to your father had to be the most awkward thing *ever*. "Um, he's thirty-six years old, tall, handsome, smart, and …" She blew a deep breath and blurted out, "He's American."

"Worse than a wanker, an American wanker. *Pah!*" Her father brought his glass down on the table with a thump. "Are there no Frenchmen here in Singapore? I didn't know *l'Ambassade de France* had closed."

"You know very well it's still there. Maybe not the same place where you worked thirty-one years ago, but yes, there are still French people in the country. I just don't like them as much as I like Aidan."

"You're breaking your father's heart with every word you say. Fine, where does he work, this American paragon of virtue who has *bite molle*."

Maddie had to laugh at her papa saying Aidan had a "soft prick." The reality was so far from it. Soft and Aidan did not match. "I'm not going to discuss that with you. Behave, or I won't tell you anymore."

"*Bon, d'accord*. I'll stop. What's his full name, and what does he do for work? Is he a client of yours?"

"No, but his younger brother is. We met in Boracay last year. His full name is Aidan Ryan, a lieutenant colonel in the US Air Force. He's the acting senior defense officer—" She broke off when her father's face turned ashen upon hearing Aidan's rank. He threw a panicked look at the open doorway and made a grab for his briefcase.

"I'm happy for you, *ma fille*. I have forgotten that I promised to meet a former colleague tonight. I'm going to have to cut our evening short." He opened the case and took out a sheaf of papers. "I've also forgotten to share my good news with you. Vivien is *enceinte*. I'm about to become a papa again."

Sweating profusely, holding out a shaking hand full of documents, her father didn't have the look of a man imparting good news.

"*Félicitations*, Papa. Am I going to have a brother or a sister?" Her suddenly constricted chest ached. She wanted one too, as she'd told Aidan last night. Their child. A sturdy little boy with her light brown eyes and his Grecian nose, perfectly straight, unlike her upturned one.

"*Merci.* It's a boy. That's one of the reasons I came to see you. I must secure his future. I need you to transfer your account to me, so he is taken care of." Taking to his feet in a rush, he handed her the papers and a pen.

With a puzzled frown she accepted the documents and gave them a quick perusal. It was all in French. Words like *transfert de fonds*, *le déclarant*, and *retirer* jumped out at her. "What account? I didn't know I had one."

Her father fanned himself with one hand while tugging at the collar of his shirt with the other, his gaze flitting from the paper to the door. "I opened it in your name to enable you to become a French citizen, and I've been making deposits on your behalf so you'll have money if I die. My wife gets the life insurance. You needed it then, but you're a success now. You don't need it anymore. I do. For your brother. Please sign and initial where marked." Papa paced beside her, occasionally wiping his face with a monogrammed handkerchief.

Maddie had signed plenty of paperwork when they'd applied for her French nationality certificate. She hadn't understood most of it, as she'd only just started learning the language. She scanned the documents she held now, her eyebrows rising at what she read. A numbered Swiss bank account in her name. How much money was in there to justify a heavily protected Swiss vault instead of a regular French bank? To stall while she attempted to understand the French jargon, she asked, "It says here we need a witness; do you want me to call the maître d'?"

"No!" her father yelled, then softened his tone. "*Pas besoin*. I'll have my lawyer notarize it when I return to Paris."

"*Mais*, Papa, isn't that going to invalidate the documents?" Surely he knew this.

"Madeleine, *s'il te plaît*, if you love me at all, please sign the papers."

Maddie's mind raced in an attempt to remember a time when her proud father had ever begged. Never in the thirteen years she'd known him. "You know I love you. What's going on? Are you in trouble?"

"*Oui*. I'm being blackmailed. I need to pay, or I will be ruined. *Mon ange*, please stop asking questions. Knowing more will endanger you. That is why I can't see you anymore after tonight. I don't want you to be used against me."

"Papa, I can't abandon you in your time of need. Maybe Aidan can help—"

"*Non!* You can't help. No one can. Least of all your fucking American military boyfriend. He's the one who got me in trouble in the first place."

Aidan did? "What are you talking about? Papa, you're scaring me. Please calm down."

"Don't ask me to keep calm. My life depends on this," he all but wailed.

This was getting more and more bizarre. His stories kept changing. Which was it? "Please sit down, Papa. I'll take a look and sign once I understand what it is I'm giving up." She meant the words to pacify; they enraged him instead.

Hazel eyes now green and blazing with fury, his skin mottled with red streaks, Jean-Marc screamed into her face, "*Tu es une ingrate.* I saved you. I provided for you when you were in need. Now you want to steal from me? Give me my fucking money!"

He continued to heap abuse upon her, but Maddie was no longer listening. She pushed her chair back from the table with so much force, it crashed to the floor. She staggered several steps away from her father, unable to be physically close to someone who savaged her because of money. Heart racing from mounting anger, she confronted the man who she'd thought before tonight loved her unconditionally. Her chest tightened, making it difficult to breathe. To speak. But she needed to know.

"*Combien*, Papa? How much am I worth? I want to know how rich I actually am before you take it all back. My money, my respect and love for you. How much, Papa?" Her voice broke at the last question. So did her heart. Her father's image was blurred from behind the film of tears that filled her eyes after his hurtful accusations.

"Close to twelve million euros," a familiar voice announced. Aidan entered the room, two other black-suited men behind him. The flags pinned on their lapels proclaimed one of them American, the other French.

"Jean-Marc Duvall is being paid one million every year for information he traded with enemies of the US, some of them with ties to terrorist organizations," Aidan said. "The payouts were deposited to your account at the end of your annual visits." His accusations were directed at her father, but he spoke only to her.

"You betrayed me, Madeleine. You led my enemies to me." Turning to the suits, Jean-Marc screamed, "You cannot take me. I'm a diplomat."

The shorter of the two men, the Frenchman, stepped forward. "Monsieur Duvall, the government of Singapore has declared you *persona non grata* for spying on an ally. You will remain in custody at the French embassy until arrangements are finalized for your escorts to accompany you to Paris."

All the bravado left him; Jean-Marc deflated before her eyes. Head bowed, shoulders slumped, he let himself be led away.

"*Adieu*, Papa," Maddie whispered, wiping her tears away. Her greatest fear had materialized. She'd lost her father, but not as she had imagined. This was worse. So much worse.

"Maddie."

All because of this man, her lover for the past ten weeks. Aidan had used her to get Jean-Marc. She'd told him where they were having dinner. With no regard for her feelings, he'd taken her father away. She'd trusted him and he'd betrayed her.

Betrayed.

"*As far as I'm concerned, there are only two reasons for us to end our relationship before our mutually agreed timeline: disloyalty and betrayal of trust.*"

Their relationship ended tonight.

With her Ma's passing, Maddie had thought she knew how the heart could break and still keep beating. She knew nothing. This pain, this hurt—there was no getting through this. This felt like death.

Dry-eyed, Maddie picked up her bag from the floor and removed a few hundred dollars to pay for their meal. Was that enough? Maybe a hundred more. She had twelve million euros in a Swiss bank; she could afford it. *Ha.* She had no intention of touching that blood money.

She shouldered her bag and faced the two men who had stayed behind. "I take it you have to take me in for questioning?" She addressed the dark-skinned man beside Aidan.

"Yes, Ms. Duvall. We appreciate your cooperation. It'll go a long way towards a favorable decision about your case." He offered her a kind smile before stepping out of the room.

Aidan blocked her way before she could follow. "Maddie, I'm sorry."

She met his eyes. "My name is Madeleine Duvall, Colonel Ryan. I'm Maddie only to my friends. You are not one of them. Excuse me, I have to clear my name." She waited for him to step aside. She left without looking back.

She couldn't look back.

If she did, she'd shatter into pieces.

I'm broken.

CHAPTER EIGHTEEN

Chiong [chong], v. – In Hokkien: to run; to rush.

Hurry! Hurry! Hurry! Aidan leaned forward in his seat. He needed to get home quickly, to catch Maddie if she was still there.

He'd had to witness several hours of Jean-Marc Duvall's interrogation. The Defense Intelligence Agency had documented all of the French diplomat's criminal activities, but it had still taken a while for the FBI agent and his French counterpart to get him to confess.

Maddie had been released and escorted home two hours before Aidan had left the building. She'd surrendered the account to the French government. It was evidence now. He figured Maddie had gone to their Tanglin apartment to pack.

Maddie. She'd said he wasn't allowed to call her that. They were not friends. Hearing her say that had been worse than a shot in the back. The bullet was still inside him, destroying his heart. He was in agony. His entire being was in throbbing, bleeding pain.

He'd chosen duty over her. It was that or break direct orders. Now, he wasn't sure it was worth it. Not when he'd lost the woman he loved. The only woman he'd been planning to spend all his tomorrows with.

Finally home, he had his seatbelt off and the door opened before the car came to a complete stop. He shouted his thanks to the driver and ran to the gate, which was promptly opened by the Malay security guard.

"Good evening, Colonel Ryan." The uniformed guard saluted.

Aidan automatically returned the salute even though he wasn't in uniform. He passed the guardhouse with long strides.

"Sir, you have visitors," the guard called after him.

Fuck. He didn't have time for this now. He turned around, scowling. "Who?" he barked at the hapless guard, who flinched at his rude tone. "*Maaf.* It's past two in the morning, and I'm tired. Who and where are they?"

"Mr. Blake Ryan and Ms. Krista Lopez are in your unit. I checked off their names against the approved visitors list. They had a key they told me they got from Ms. Duvall, but I still escorted them."

Maddie isn't here. He flinched as the jagged shrapnel in his chest grazed tender flesh. "What time did they arrive?"

"One-fifty, sir."

Not too long ago. He thanked the guard with a nod and walked to the elevators, his shoulders slumped.

Maddie had left him. Aidan wanted to howl at the loss. He smashed his fist against the elevator panel instead. He felt nothing. Broken circles grooved his knuckles from the buttons, but he still didn't feel anything. He was numb from head to toe. Drained.

He pushed the door to his apartment open. With Maddie gone, he no longer had a home. Without her in it, this place was just a shelter.

The first thing he saw was Blake wrapping a tall ceramic urn in old newspapers. His brother had taken the prints off the wall and had rolled up the rugs.

Aidan snatched the vase away from his younger brother and cradled it close to his chest. "You're not taking away anything from my place."

Blake gaped at him. "Aidan, these are Maddie's things."

"If she wants them, she has to get them herself."

"Aren't you being unreasonable?"

"No." Aidan unwrapped the ceramic and placed it back where Maddie had put it before, on top of the rectangular dining table. He'd get the rest later. He headed to the bedroom to stop Krista. If she wasn't in the living room, she had to be in there packing Maddie's things.

Blake blocked his way. "She's mad at you. Be careful how you respond. I won't have you intimidating my future wife."

They were the same height. Blake was bulkier, but Aidan was confident he could handle himself in a fight. Not right now, though. His knuckles had started to throb. "Step aside, Blake. This is my house. You're the trespassers here."

He had no intention of hurting Krista's feelings. All he wanted was for them to leave so he could nurse his guilt and pain. Alone. Preferably wrapped in sheets that smelled of Maddie.

Instead of stepping aside, Blake entered the bedroom ahead of him.

Aidan nearly dropped to his knees at the sight before him. The bed was stripped of its linens. A suitcase partially filled with dresses, shoes, and toiletries inside clear bags lay on top of the bare mattress. Those were fine. Krista could take those. Maddie needed them for work. But not the gray stilettos, and not their bed sheets. *He* needed those.

Aidan turned left and right but couldn't find the red silk set anywhere in the room. *The suitcase.* He tossed its contents to the floor until he got to the bottom, where his bedding was neatly folded. "Thank fuck." He exhaled a relieved sigh.

Pushing the suitcase off, he set about remaking the bed.

"Aidan, what are you doing?" Krista screamed at him. She came out of the walk-in closet with an armful of clothes and dropped them on the suitcase.

"Go away, Krista. Take what you've got there and leave. If Madeleine needs anything else, she can call me and I'll take them to her. Or, she can come home where she belongs."

Krista's answer was to tug on one corner. He threw her an angry glare. She responded in kind.

"Let go."

She straightened and pointed a finger at him. "No, Aidan. You don't get to order me around. You don't get to sound as if you're the aggrieved party. I told you in Boracay that Maddie only acts tough, and I asked you to take care of her. But what did you do? You hurt her instead. How could you?"

"Easy, baby." Blake stood beside his fiancée and took her in his arms.

Two against one. Three, including Maddie. Nobody was on his side. He guessed he deserved it; Krista was right. He had promised. Head bowed, Aidan fisted the top sheet. "I'm sorry."

Krista sighed and dropped onto the bed. "Do you know what you did when you caused her to lose her father? You orphaned her. She transferred all her love for her Ma to him after she died. Now, it's as if he's dead too."

He let go of the sheet and sat beside Maddie's best friend. "I know, Krista. You're not telling me anything I haven't already been beating myself up for."

"Maddie loved you, and you broke her heart."

Loved. Past tense? "I love her too." He should have told Maddie first, not her best friend.

Tears shone in Krista's eyes. "I thought you did, but you clearly don't. Because if you loved her, you would have found another way to capture Jean-Marc Duvall. You would have shielded Maddie from being hurt by her own father. You would have warned her so she could prepare herself. So, no. You don't love Maddie. You love your duty, but not Maddie."

Aidan jumped to his feet. "Enough," he roared, earning him a shouted, "Hey," from Blake. He continued in a gentler tone. "You weren't there. Madeleine wasn't outside to see the other agents forcibly holding me back as soon as her father started the lies. I wanted to wrap my hands around his neck and twist it until he died. They only let me go when I promised to keep my focus on her and not her father."

He flexed his hands. They'd curled into claws as he imagined squeezing the life out of Duvall. "I had no right to be there at all. The arrest wasn't part of my job. I went there to protect Maddie. To comfort her, because I knew what her father wanted from her, and I couldn't tell her. She would have warned him not to come."

Krista took an eternity to respond. When she did, her voice was somber. "You're a Scorpio, Aidan. You should have known the thing that hurts us the most is being lied to by people we love. If you really love Maddie, you'll stay away from her until she recovers from the pain you and her father dealt her."

Everything in Aidan protested at the mere thought of that, even though it was exactly what he feared Maddie wanted him to do. He pivoted and banged his fist against the wall. His already-injured fist was now a grotesque misshapen blob. "I can't stay away." But he should, perhaps for a couple of days. At most, a week. He could give her that much.

He turned around to meet their gazes. "I will leave Madeleine alone to heal for now. But at some point, I will seek her out and ask her to forgive me and give me another chance. I will never give up on her. On us."

Blake stepped forward and clapped a hand on his shoulder. "Good luck, big brother. You're going to need it. Whatever happens, we're here for you. For both of you."

Aidan nodded at his brother, grateful for the support. He shifted his gaze to Krista, who offered a shrug.

"Come on, I'll bandage your hand and then Blake and I will go back to Maddie. She's hurting."

Krista didn't seem completely convinced, but she was giving him the benefit of the doubt. Aidan hoped Maddie would do the same. If she gave him one chance, he would seize it and prove to her that he loved her. Just one chance. All he needed.

CHAPTER NINETEEN

Gone case, adv. – In Singlish: irredeemable; irreparable; not rectifiable; too far gone.

"Did you get them?" Maddie asked Krista as soon as she opened the door. Her heart sank when she received a head shake. She stepped to the side to let the engaged couple in, dragging two of her suitcases behind them. Still, she pounced on her bags to check for the one thing she'd asked for: her favorite red silk bedsheets. The ones she'd bought when Aidan was in Thailand. Krista wouldn't lie, but she had to know for sure.

Her head dropped when her friend's negative response was confirmed. They weren't in the bags. Still kneeling on the floor, she looked up at the pair.

"Aidan found the bedsheets in the suitcase and remade the bed. He went berserk, Mads," Krista said, wide-eyed.

"Berserk?" Maddie jumped to her feet, shaking her head, finding it difficult to associate the word with Aidan. He was the epitome of control.

Krista nodded. "Yes. He wouldn't let us take anything except some of your clothes and shoes. He kept the dark gray stilettos. Held them to his chest like they were precious." Krista looked to her fiancé to add to the tale.

"Aidan's knuckles were swollen and bleeding. He punched the wall in the bedroom, but even before that he was already injured. He must have hit the elevator panel coming up when he realized you'd left him. A couple of the buttons were cracked. The guard must have told him we were there, instead of you."

Maddie's heart stuttered for a second. "Is he okay?" she asked.

"Not really, but he'll live." After another unspoken communication with his fiancée, Blake continued. "He wanted to come here, but we told him to give you space. He promised to stay away, but not for long. Maybe a week or two, if I know my brother. He won't give you up, Maddie."

Maddie hardened her heart against any threads of sympathy for her former lover. She headed for the sofa. "Your brother used me to get to my father. He gained access to my data through that background check and by snooping on my electronics." How else could he have gotten ahold of her detailed receipts and itineraries? He'd warned her about protecting her password, but only after he'd already snooped. He'd lied to her.

Krista sat beside her. "Aidan said he loves you, and I believe him."

Maddie had believed he did too, especially last night when he'd made love to her so tenderly. She thought she'd heard him say, "I love you." Clearly, she'd dreamt it.

Voice tight, she said, "He broke our first rule. We'd promised to be honest with each other. He's been lying to me for more than two weeks." It was *that* day at Palawan Beach. Aidan's claim of wanting a change of scenery had been a lie. They'd gone there for his meeting with General MacCormack. Seventeen days: that was how long it had been since he knew about her father's espionage. He'd kept it from her for that length of time. They'd slept together for twelve nights since his return from Hawaii, and he hadn't shown her he trusted her to do the right thing.

"If you'd known about Aidan's mission, would you have helped him capture your papa, or would you have told your father not to come to Singapore?" Krista asked quietly.

A sharp ache shot from Maddie's ripped heart. She rubbed it away with the pad of her palm. In vain, for that pain would take forever to heal.

Jean-Marc Duvall was another Big Ken. He was a thief of top secret US information. Her father was a spy, the bad kind. Not like the Hollywood hero Rini thought Aidan was. Her papa had used her. He'd been using her to gain ill-gotten wealth for almost half her life. Did he love her at all?

She let her head fall back on the sofa. It ached from too much crying and from asking herself questions she didn't know how to answer. Like the one her best friend had asked.

Without moving her head, Maddie replied. "I don't know, Kris. I would have demanded proof before I made my decision, and I'm not sure if Aidan would have been able to provide that." This was her problem. Despite her hurt, she had to be fair. She couldn't demonize Aidan. Both Hui Min and Trisha had advised her weeks ago about accepting secrecy as part of her life now that she was a partner to a military officer. Easy in theory, not so much in practice.

The FBI guy had told her before he released her from the interrogation that Colonel Ryan had already proven she wasn't an accomplice to her father's crimes. Nevertheless, they had to go through her interview to fulfill proper procedures.

Her brain understood all that.

Her heart ... It was still shattered. It did not understand logic.

"Maddie." A deep male voice said her name.

Aidan! She sat straight up, only to slump back when she saw it was Blake crouched before her, holding out a folded sheet of paper.

"Aidan wanted me to give this to you. It might not be legible. His hand was pretty beat up. He could barely hold the pen."

She took it from his fingers and stared at her name written in Aidan's aggressive scrawl. *Madeleine.* She closed her eyes against the burning sensation that threatened tears. She'd told him not to call her Maddie. He'd complied. She wished he hadn't.

She opened her eyes at Krista's touch on her arm. "Mads, please rest. It's past three. You're exhausted. I can hold on to the letter if you're not ready to read it yet."

"No," Maddie snapped. She clutched the paper tightly, flinching as the edge sliced her palm. What was a tiny paper cut compared to what she'd already suffered tonight? "I'll keep it," she said in a gentler tone. "Please go to bed, both of you. Don't change your plans today for my sake. I can't join you for lunch, but maybe we can meet at the Gardens by the Bay in the afternoon." She stood to forestall their protests. "Thanks for going to—" She broke off, unable to say his name. "For bringing my things back. 'Night."

With the little reserve of energy remaining in her body, she walked to her bedroom. A turtle could have passed her, but she made it without stumbling or falling flat on her face.

She laid the letter on the bedside table. She'd read it in a bit, but first, a pain reliever. Wine or paracetamol? *Ha! Who am I kidding?* She didn't drink; she'd only throw up.

Two tablets later, she unfolded the paper. A sob burst out of her at the sight of the first line. Tears fell unrestrained as she read.

Dear Maddie,

I'm sorry. For stealing the privilege of using the name only your friends call you. You may no longer consider me your friend, but I will always think of you as mine.

I'm sorry for letting my job take precedence over you. It was never my intention to hurt you, yet my choices took away yours. I will give up my career if it means having you by my side and in my arms again.

I'm sorry for my selfishness in holding on to your things. As long as they remain with me, I have hope that you'll return.

I'm sorry my words are inadequate to express my regret for hurting you. I will wait until you grant me the opportunity to say it in person and seek your forgiveness and love.

Always yours,
Aidan

CHAPTER TWENTY

Ta pau [tah pow], v. – In Mandarin: to bag up take away food.

"Eleven twenty-nine." Maddie glanced at her phone to confirm the time. He should be here soon. He came every Saturday morning, eleven thirty on the dot. Today marked the eighth week. *Ooh, maybe I should open the door a bit so I can hear his footsteps.* Nope. She didn't want to look too eager. Like standing behind the front door, straining to listen to sounds from outside didn't make her look foolish.

She unlocked the door. He'd arrive any second now.

Should she wait for a knock first? She did last week. It was time to change things up, confuse him.

Oh, wait. She heard a thud of something heavy being set down on the floor. That meant go time. She reached for the handle with one hand and into her shorts with the other.

"Ta-da!" A five-foot-nothing dynamo wearing a manic smile and flashing jazz hands stood on her doorstep.

"Gie? You're early. Where is — *Oof!*" The force of the hug took her a couple of steps back. "Are you training for sumo wrestling? You'll win, hands down." She extricated herself from her friend's encircling arms to peek into the hallway. No one else was there. But she could swear she smelled it.

Angela reached for her backpack—the cause of the thud Maddie had heard a moment ago—and dragged it in, kicking the door closed behind her. "Against you, yes. That's because a gentle puff of breeze would blow you away. You're malnourished, ma bitch."

Maddie rolled her eyes at the deliberate mangling of the French endearment *ma biche* for "my dear." Angela knew how to pronounce it properly: *ma beesh*. Her friend had been that way since college. In their French class, she'd always pretended to mispronounce words when they were first taught, but when testing came, she'd spoken it like a native.

"What happened to Ange? Why are you calling me Gie now? That's Krista's nickname for me, not yours." Angela spoke from her seat on the couch, booted feet on the arm, thankfully not on the glass-topped coffee table.

"I didn't know there was a patent on nicknames now," Maddie replied absently, half of her attention outside. She opened the door again and stuck her head out to check for her expected visitor. Still not there. Should she call his mobile? Maybe there'd been an accident.

"Looking for this?" Angela held the familiar paper bag of goodness aloft. It had been in the backpack.

Maddie snatched the bag away. "This is why I don't call you Ange anymore. You're no angel." She headed to the dining table to unload her favorite meal from its delivery containers, quickly hiding the folded note she knew held the lines, *I'm sorry. I miss you.*

She'd set the table hours ago. For one. If Angela really insisted on having some, she could get her own plates and cutlery or eat with her hands from the disposable paper that enwrapped the food.

"You're the best hostess in the world. Look at this spread to welcome me to your home. Hainanese chicken rice, my homeland's best dish. *Shiok!*" As Maddie expected, Angela helped herself to the food, even the skin Maddie had removed when she'd taken her own portion.

Pulling the plate of *kailan* closer, she frowned at her friend. "This is all for me. I didn't know you were coming this early. You didn't give me your flight details."

"Yeah, that best hostess bit was sadcasm. Sarcasm wasted on you. No wonder Krista is worried. You're off your game, babe. Still pining for Alphahole Aidan?"

She was. "Of course not. I'm over him. I've moved on." Not. She stuffed some chicken into her mouth before she uttered more lies.

Angela gave a loud snort. "Right. That's why you're scarfing down the meal he had delivered for you like it's the only thing you eat all week."

Pretty spot on. But how—?

"Your delivery boy was closemouthed at first, but I used my investigative reporting *skeelz* on him. Both of you overtip him, you know. Two hundred percent. Should be zero *lah*."

Maddie knew tipping wasn't mandatory here in Singapore. But Aidan had always been a generous tipper. He was thrifty with everything else except for her perfume and rewarding those who served him personally. Efficient servers received twenty percent. Exceptional ones up to thirty. Safe drivers not only had the fare rounded off, they also got an extra five. Vik, the enterprising South Asian teenager who delivered her food, received extra because he was their main connection. Plus, the chicken rice was not expensive to begin with.

"Did you tip the kid?" She touched the bank note in her pocket. If Angela hadn't, she would double his next tip.

"Of course. What do you take me for? Granted?"

"Har-har-har. I'm serious. How much did you give him? He deserves it, you know. He rides his motorcycle to Tanglin to meet Aidan, then to Maxwell Road to *ta pau* the meal before coming all the way here to the East Coast to deliver it to me."

"Relax. I gave him ten. Sheesh."

Maddie pulled out the yellow legal tender, which had the image of the country's first president on it and handed it to Angela. She went back to finishing her meal. If Angela hadn't been here, she'd have taken her time savoring every mouthful. Today, she didn't have the luxury of dipping into her happy memories of eating with Aidan.

"Twenty? *Alamak!* I'll be *pok kai* if I do the same as you. When I lived here, this whole meal cost less than five."

"When was that? Last millennium?" Madeleine had to smile at her friend's over the top reactions.

"At the turn." Angela hooted with laughter. "*Uuuy*, your humor is returning. *Yehey!*"

"I told you, I'm fine." Maddie stood to clear the table. "I can't remember a time when Singapore wasn't one of the most expensive places to live in the world."

Angela followed her to the kitchen. "Chicken rice was definitely cheaper when I was a baby. When I came back to do my Oath of Renunciation, Allegiance, and Loyalty after I turned twenty-one—which was, yikes, ten years ago—stuff was already super *mahal*. That's why I can't live here with what I earn." She dumped the trash and stood beside Maddie at the sink. "Here, give it to your delivery boy." She placed the twenty under a mug. "When's his next visit?"

"Tomorrow morning at eight."

"Sweeeet! What is he bringing next?"

"*Kaya* toast breakfast with *kopi o kosong*." Maddie led the way back to the living room.

"*Wah lao!* I want *teh tarik*." Angela made a slurping sound. "Wait! Does he come every day? If he does, how come you're stick thin?"

"Not daily. Only on weekends." If she had overseas trips, she made sure to come home by Friday night at the latest. So far, she'd been lucky to keep those conferences to Southeast Asia. "Stop calling me stick thin. You exaggerate."

Before they could sit, Angela caught Maddie's arm and held it beside hers. "Tell me what you see."

Two limbs: one golden brown, toned and gleaming with health, the other pale and bony. "I see you need a better moisturizer. I have samples here. I'll give you some." Maddie drew her arm back to her side and sank down on the couch. So she was fine-boned. Blame Irene.

Angela the Relentless bounced beside her. "Ha ha. Not funny. I'll take the beauty products, thanks. You, however, need your eyes checked. You're almost a foot taller than me, but our arms are the same size. It's because I'm in fantastic shape. You, *m'amie*, are not."

"I've been busy. Lots of work. I travel a lot. It rains every day."

"Excuses, excuses. Ever heard of a gym? I'm sure this place, as *atas* as it is, has one. Yoga? Dance? Indoor rock climbing? Boxing?"

Aidan did yoga. Did he still? She'd bumped into Noir at Orchard the week after their breakup, but they'd only waved to each other. He and Hui Min had probably already heard what had happened. They were also likely on his side.

Maddie drew a sigh. Good thing she had her own dear friends. Like this chatterbox in her flat right now, who was still extolling the virtues of proper diet and regular exercise. "You're opening and closing your mouth, but I can't hear a word you're saying. Lalalalala."

Angela flung a pillow at her. She caught and embraced it. "I don't understand why people punish themselves when they get their hearts broken. I'm guessing you don't eat anything except what Alphahole sends you."

"I eat, I just don't have much of an appetite." Not for food, nor for shopping, and definitely not for other men.

She missed Aidan.

She missed their talks, the sharing of personal stories.

She missed his massages. Her perfume and scented oils remained unopened. They didn't bring her joy anymore because he wasn't here to smell them and get turned on by them, or by her.

She missed making love with him. They'd never made love here, so she didn't have those memories to draw on as inspiration when her body needed relief.

The click of a camera brought Maddie out of her memories and back into the present.

"You're thinking of him. You got all violin music and sepia-toned all of a sudden," Angela observed, her words teasing, her expression sympathetic. "You've forgiven Aidan, haven't you? You still love him."

"I have. I do." There was no use denying the truth.

Angela waited for her to elaborate, but she remained silent, so her friend moved on to another topic. "How about the other *connard*? Dear old Papa Duvall. You seem to be shedding off the French these days. I haven't heard a '*chérie*' or a 'shit *de la merde*' from you in a while."

A faint twinge poked her heart. "We haven't talked at all since that night. The FBI agent who worked the case told me he had been stripped of his diplomatic credentials. He's probably in hiding, in some kind of witness protection program."

Her father hadn't been allowed to contact her, but anonymous updates had begun appearing in her personal e-mail and in her mailbox since early April. First was the information that Jean-Marc had opened the account to provide for her, as he'd told her at dinner. Next were the threats on her life if he didn't continue to obtain American strategies. Most recently, there'd been news about the dismantling of several terrorist organizations that had bought classified data.

Maddie suspected Aidan had sent those updates. It was one of his many ways of atonement that went a long way in mending the rip in her heart.

"As for the French, I'm taking a break from that part of my heritage. I'm not working with a French client right now, and there's a new boss, a Brahmin, so I'll only look pretentious if I keep dropping *d'accords* all over the place."

Angela's face contorted in a cross-eyed, crinkled-nose, twisted-lip comical mask. Gurgles rattled in her throat.

"What's wrong with you? Don't hold that look for too long, or it might become permanent."

Angela exploded into a raucous laughter. "Do you ... remember ... college ..." She could barely speak from laughing.

Maddie buried her face in her hands and groaned. She knew where Angela was going with this.

"You had your name changed, and after only one sem, you were *parlez vous*-ing *français* like you thought you were Audrey Tautou."

"*Aaaargh!* I was such a poseur."

Angela sobered. In a serious tone, she said. "In fairness, you never once broke character. Through the years, you've grown into the role of Madeleine Duvall so completely, we can no longer remember you were Maddie Estrella before."

"Is that a good thing though? When I became French, did I totally give up my Filipino identity?"

Angela tilted her head to the side in a pose of contemplation. "Well, you never used to eat rice or pork, even before you became a French citizen, so it's not as if you were a full-fledged Filipino to begin with."

"Ange!"

"Aaand, she's back!" Her friend clapped her hands upon hearing her preferred nickname. "Just telling it like it is. I think that's why the three of us—you, Krista, and me—gravitated towards one another. We're all part but separate."

Too true. The three of them were part of the Philippines, but their mixed heritage separated them from most of the country. They were multiracial, half-half. Not completely one or the other. "You're so wise, *m'amie*. I'm glad you're here." Maddie leaned over to give her friend a hug.

"Thanks for having me. I'll be here all week." She said it the same way comedians on TV often did.

"Really? Um—" Maddie pretended to look worried. She didn't mind if Angela stayed longer.

"Don't look too alarmed. I won't overstay my welcome. I'll go back to Manila as soon as I get my new passport. Then to Koh Samui after that."

"Is it your month there again? How is swapping places with your business partner working out for both of you?"

"Good. He's improving his English, and I'm crushing on someone." A becoming blush colored Angela's sun-kissed cheeks.

"Ooh! I'd love to hear this."

"Not yet. I'm ... Hmm ... Can I tell you when I'm ready? I want to keep him my naughty little secret for a little while longer."

Early days of attraction. They burned hot and bright. "Sure. I understand completely."

"Don't tell Krista, *ha*? She keeps wanting to introduce me to Blake's brother, and after your drama with Alphahole, I'm not too enthusiastic about catching a ride on the Ryan bandwagon, even if it's the last trip to nirvana."

"Stop calling Aidan that." Maddie didn't put much heat in her admonition. At this point, it had become almost like an endearment. She'd labeled him that in the first place.

"Oh, right. You love the arrogant ass."

"Not that, either."

"Okay, okay. See what I mean? So, when are you getting back together?"

"I don't know. I guess it's my move to give him the signal that I'm ready to talk."

"What are you waiting for? Whatever happened to *carpe diem*? Wasn't that how your relationship started? He asked the first day you met again, and you said yes right away."

Maddie stared at her friend with unseeing eyes. What happened to that Maddie? To Mad. She used to be decisive, used to love speed. She'd loved Colonel I-Fly because he moved as fast as her old Porsche. This Maddie was sad, boring. She had to bring Mad back.

She blinked and with new resolve, she answered Angela. "You're right. It's time."

"All right! One thing, though. Before you go to your big reconciliation extravaganza, you have to put some meat on your bones and color in your cheeks, first. Oh-kay?"

Maddie nodded meekly. "*Opo, Ate*," she teased, calling her five-months-older friend by the Filipino term of respect for older sister.

"You know what? Since I'm here, let's start now." Angela jumped to her feet and lifted her backpack by the straps. "That my room?" She pointed to the open door to the right of the hall bathroom.

Maddie nodded, standing as well. "What do you mean 'now'?"

"We're going out. Bask in the sun and eat, after I change into shorts."

"We already ate."

"Not enough. We shared the chicken rice, a one-person meal. I'm hungry again."

"For a tiny thing, you eat a lot. You should be with a chef."

"Not you too! Tell you what. If it doesn't work out with my grizzly bear, I'll meet this Craig person you and Krista keep trying to foist on me."

Grizzly bear? Wasn't Craig supposed to be huge and hairy? Could it be? It would be funny if they were the same person. Serve the bossy little baggage right. "Deal."

***

"Mads, don't turn around. There's a couple of people from the US team who are looking at you super-serious," Angela warned her. Maddie grinned at her friend's suspicious tone. The fantastic morning weather—cool and bright—and the presence of her old and new friends made her cheerful, despite the aches and pains she was beginning to feel after engaging in unfamiliar exercise.

This was exactly what she'd hoped for when she suggested they join the Philippine team for practice at the crack of dawn this Sunday morning here on the Kallang River. She'd expected Hui Min and Noir and their respective spouses to be here. Even though they'd remained friends after her breakup with Aidan, she hadn't engaged them on social media. But she'd stalked their pages until she found the correct location. Dragon boat racers practiced in three areas: Bedok Reservoir, Marina Channel, and here. It was Angela, however, who'd snagged the invitation to paddle with the other Filipino residents in the country.

Defying her friend, Maddie turned towards the people who could help her reconcile with Aidan.

She'd only taken two steps on the pebbly riverbank before Hui Min came running.

"Maddie! I missed you." The smaller woman hugged her much like Angela had yesterday: bone-crushing and literally breath-stealing.

"I missed you too, Hui Min." She patted the other woman's shoulder and smiled at Noir, who was approaching more sedately. No longer the whitest man in Singapore, he'd obviously embraced the sun worship of his current home.

"Hey, babe." He gave her a peck on the cheek. "Lovely to see you. It's been so long."

"I know. It's great to see you too. How have you been?" She had to observe the niceties, but all she wanted was to ask about Aidan.

"Good *lah*. Although, my husband is very not," Hui Min startled her by saying.

"What's wrong with Kalvin?" Maddie glanced over at the lanky redheaded naval chief petty officer, who was the image of the local word for foreigner—*ang moh*.

"He can't wait for Aidan to be re-assigned. Your ex has been the crankiest, most demanding commander, ever since you left."

Re-assigned? She was too late! Heart in her throat, Maddie croaked, "Aidan is leaving? When?"

Hui Min looked around before leaning forward and whispering, "I'm not supposed to tell you this, but I saw a form for return to service on the ambassador's desk. That means one of the military attachés is being called back to the US. I didn't see the name, but it has Colonel Ryan's signature on it."

Heart beating three times faster than it had been a second ago, Maddie shook her head frantically. "No! He said one year." But he'd said it in January. He'd also said in his letter that he'd wait.

"It might not be him," Hui Min blurted. "Like I said, I'm not sure—"

"Do you want him back, darling?" Noir asked, cutting off Hui Min. "Maybe we can help." He tucked her to his side.

"He's away right now, back on Friday night. We can't do anything until Saturday," Hui Min supplied.

"Maddie! See you next Sunday?" someone from the Philippine team asked when they passed by.

That's it! She grabbed her two embassy friends' arms as she replied, "I'll be here."

"We'll take care of it. He'll be here too," Noir promised.

Hui Min jumped up and down. "Yay!"

She hugged them both and called out to Angela, who'd moved to chat with some people who still lingered. "Ange, let's go."

"Where to?" her friend asked when she reached Maddie's side.

"We're getting a new tattoo."

"What about breakfast? You told Vik yesterday to bring *teh tarik* for me. It's almost eight. Let's go home first."

"Of course we're eating breakfast first, glutton."

"Then why did you say the tattoo thing?"

"Because I'm excited. I'm going to see Aidan again, Ange. It's time to *carpe diem*."

"Seize the day," her friend yelled, making them both laugh uproariously.

Power. Control. Speed. Maddie recalled the mantra.

It was time to reclaim her old self.

It's time to become Mad again.

CHAPTER TWENTY-ONE

Kan cheong [khan chawng], adv. – In Hokkien: nervous.

Aidan stood on the bank, watching silver streaks of light succeed in their valiant attempt to burst through the dawn sky. The gray water of the river acted as a perfect mirror. His gaze moved lower, to the currently empty, multicolored paddled long boats parked at the edge of the water. Decorated with their respective country's national symbol, they were lined up in a row: team USA's stars and stripes, Australia's green and gold, Thailand's purple, and Malaysia's crescent and star. Noticeably absent was the red, white, blue, and yellow boat he sought. Later, twenty rowers, one drummer, and one steer person would compete to propel each to the finish line in the fastest time.

Right now, one hour before the start of the race, Aidan questioned the veracity of the intel that had brought him here. Madeleine, his Maddie, was supposed to have joined team Philippines for training last weekend and had promised to return today.

The crunch of soft-soled shoes against rocky sand and the dainty figure moving into his peripheral vision alerted him to the presence of his source of that information. "She'll be here, sir," Hui Min assured him. "Maddie told me so herself."

He nodded, more in acknowledgment of her conviction rather than any real agreement on his part. The Maddie he knew had been waking up early, that was true, but never on Sunday, and never at five in the morning to be able to get here at five thirty. She'd luxuriated in their bed, gloriously naked, until he'd either divested himself of his sweats and rejoined her there or picked her up in his arms to deposit her in the shower. Both choices had them not getting out of the apartment until midmorning, many times not until their stomachs protested the lack of nourishment.

The last time that had happened was nine weeks ago. He'd had nine weeks of waking up alone with morning wood that wouldn't subside until he'd wrapped his hands around it and given himself an empty release. Nine Sunday mornings of getting up lonely, determined one minute to deliver the *kaya* toast breakfast himself and deciding against it the next.

Aidan had promised Krista and Blake he would give Maddie time to heal and to forgive. He'd fulfilled that promise. Now, he was sick of it. He'd gotten tired of being patient. So, here he stood at dawn, sweat dampening his shirt courtesy of the seventy-nine-degree temperature combined with eighty-percent humidity. The not-altogether-unpleasant odors of brine, loam, and minerals crinkled his nose, and his one cup of coffee tasted bitter in his throat without the sugar from the bread he usually ate with it. All because he was told Maddie would show up at this place and time.

"*Um*, Colonel Ryan," Hui Min mumbled, drawing his attention. She was shuffling her feet and avoiding his gaze.

His stomach clenched. "She's not coming."

Hui Min raised her eyes to meet his. "She is. But, I might have made her think you're being reassigned soon. Sorry."

Aidan let out a huge breath and barked out a laugh. The tightness in his stomach eased. It hadn't occurred to him to try that. He didn't want another lie added to his sins. But he couldn't fault the repentant woman beside him for trying to help, especially if she'd succeeded in orchestrating this meeting. He patted her shoulder. "Thank you."

Hui Min smiled in relief, then ran to her husband, who flashed him a grin. He was in on the scheme too.

Noir appeared beside Aidan, two bottles of water in hand. "Here, drink some of this water. You'll be splashed with the nasty stuff later, so keep the gut clean for the Kallang special."

"Thanks." He took a swig, then practically gulped down the entire bottle. It felt like eighty-four right now, not a wisp of wind in the muggy air. The temperature here in June remained constant from five thirty to eight thirty: hot and wet. Then it got hotter and wetter after that.

"Thank *you* for coming. You're saving my hubby's incredibly fine butt today. Team USA will look good in the photos with you in them," Noir gushed.

Aidan toed a loose rock with his brand-new water shoes, uncomfortable with the undeserved praise. "Only in photos. I haven't done this before." Even though this was only practice, and some of the paddlers were newbies like him, he fully expected it to be extremely competitive.

"You'll be fine. You're fit and toned. There'll be a few practice runs before the actual race at six thirty."

"It's ten to six. Why haven't we—"

"Filipino! Filipino! *Kami panalo! Kayo talo!*"

As one, the participants turned to watch the entrance of the flamboyant group. In red shirts and blue shorts, white caps on their heads, the Philippine team arrived in style.

Aidan's whole body clenched as if readying itself for the onslaught of a powerful force. In all his life, he'd met nobody more powerful than Madeleine Duvall. His heart thundered, his senses sharpened, his attention focused on the one person who had turned his life upside down since they'd met seven months ago.

He took a couple of steps forward just as the crowd parted to reveal her walking behind her team's boat.

She's beautiful. Her hair—dyed inky black—was up in a ponytail, pulling her flawless, unmade-up skin taut over her high cheekbones.

Her body, while sexy, worried him. She was thin. Her shirt hung loosely from her shoulders and he'd seen her shorts fit her hips better before than they did now. He'd lost weight too, but not as much as Maddie had.

Aidan feared this would happen; that was why he'd arranged the regular delivery of chicken rice and *kaya* toast. It didn't look like she'd eaten it. He knew she'd accepted the food. Perhaps she gave it away as soon as Vikram left.

He should have gone himself. Taken care of her himself. Made sure she ate every bite. He stepped forward to approach Maddie, only to be brought up short when Nate, the embassy's press officer, called his name.

"Colonel Ryan, we're ready to go," Nate said. "We need you in the middle for balance."

Aidan glanced Maddie's way again. She had donned a life vest, and someone was helping her board the boat.

Fuck it. This had better be the shortest one hour of dragon boat racing in history.

***

It was the longest one hour of dragon boat racing in history. The race was finished, but their boat had yet to reach the riverbank. Team USA remained on the river because Nate insisted on taking photos for the embassy's social media pages. Maddie had better not have left by the time they disembarked, or the State Department would be one press officer short.

"Nate, man, are we done here?" He was ready to swim if necessary.

"Yes. Let's go! Can't wait to upload these," came the giddy reply.

"We only took third place. Why is he so happy?" he asked Noir, who sat to his right. The Philippine team had the best time, followed by

Australia. Both teams had left the river once the race was done.

"That's our highest finish ever. We usually come in last. You're our secret weapon." His yoga instructor was all smiles. "Although, we both know you didn't do it for the team."

No. Aidan had wanted Maddie to notice him. But he'd only caught glimpses of her, because she also sat on the left side. Every time he glanced at their boat, either his view of her was blocked by her seatmate or she was focused on the mechanics of the activity. He got caught up in the competition when the race started and concentrated on giving his best. He'd done all he could for the team, now on to winning back his woman.

Adrenaline coursed through Aidan the moment he caught sight of Maddie. He recognized her right away, even though she'd changed clothes. A large tote over her right shoulder, she stood with her back to the water, talking with a group of people. His eyes narrowed on a blond guy who was standing much too close to his girlfriend. A surfer, from the tanned skin, and the t-shirt and board shorts attire.

Aidan ripped apart the Velcro that fastened his life vest and stood abruptly. "Okay if I don't help bring the boat in? I need to go." He handed the orange safety jacket to Noir.

"Go get her, tiger."

Aidan vaulted out of the boat, unmindful of the splash he created. The group with Maddie had started to disperse. Only the surfer dude remained.

He skidded to a halt a few yards away to calm himself before he reached them. Sharp needles of jealousy pricked him. Of course the guy was asking Maddie out for a date. Who in his right mind wouldn't? She'd probably had a lot of offers in the past two months. Only Blake's and Krista's reassurance that Maddie hadn't gone out with anyone since they broke up kept him from decking the guy for even trying. He could only hope Maddie had refused.

A few discreet sniffs to ensure he didn't stink too bad and several cleansing breaths later, he was ready to go. He walked slowly, sticking to the grassy areas to muffle the sounds of his approach. As he neared, he saw the guy's cocky smile fade upon hearing Maddie say gently, "I'll see you around." The other man threw a resentful glance in Aidan's direction and turned to go.

Thank you, he mentally whispered to the heavens. He still had a chance to make things right.

He knew the exact moment Maddie decided to face him. She adjusted her hold on her bag, straightened her spine, rolled her shoulders back, and took a deep breath. Then she turned around.

"Hello, Aidan." Her hazel eyes, more brown than green, were dry, no spark. Dark half-moons shadowed beneath. The hand clutching her bag trembled.

It took all his self-control not to enfold her in his arms. When he'd imagined how they would meet again, he didn't see it being this awkward.

"Maddie-line," he fumbled, belatedly adding the third syllable of her full name. He'd been breaking her ban of not using her nickname. In his mind, they were friends. More than that, they were lovers. Still. Always.

"Maddie is ... fine," she slurred before swaying on her feet and tipping forward.

"Maddie!" Aidan caught her in his arms before she fell. His fingers sought her neck to measure her pulse rate. His mind blanked. How could he check hers when his was pounding in his chest?

"Colonel Ryan! What happened?" Hui Min rushed to his side, followed by her husband.

"Maddie fainted. Take her bag so I can lift her. Kalvin, call the driver. We have to take her to the hospital." No sooner had Hui Min complied than Aidan bent to pick up Maddie. He headed for the road with as much speed as he could without jostling her. How light she was. How frail.

"No ... hospital," Maddie whispered against his neck.

His knees nearly buckled in relief. He slowed his pace. "But you need to be seen by a doctor."

"Just hungry ... and sleepy. I called Vik while waiting for you. He's taking the food to Tanglin." She tightened her hold around his shoulders and tucked her head in the crook of his neck. "Let's go home, Aidan."

Home. With him. Where she belonged.

For the first time in nine weeks, everything was right in the world.

My Maddie is coming back home.

CHAPTER TWENTY-TWO

Lagi [lah ghee], adv. – In Malay: more, or greater than usual.

Sitting on the love seat with her feet tucked under her, Maddie eyed Aidan over the rim of her coffee mug as he paced back and forth. She'd never seen him as nervous as he was now. He'd watched her like a hawk while she ate two pieces of toast and one egg, which was all her stomach could handle—more, and she would have thrown up. It wasn't until she'd declared herself full that he began wolfing down his share of their breakfast, which was twice the amount of their usual order from Vik.

If that was his first time on a dragon boat, it was no wonder he was starved. Paddling was hard. She'd been hungry, too, last Sunday when she and Angela had gone to Kallang at the crack of dawn. Part of the "Get Maddie Some Color on Her Cheeks and Meat on Her Bones Before She Meets Aidan" project. Before she'd left for Manila yesterday, Angela had declared the project a success.

Maddie had thought so too, but today's fainting spell proved she still had a long way to go. Aidan was swoon-worthy, for sure. It didn't mean she had to literally fall at his feet. They both had some explaining to do. Starting now.

She drained her overly sweet coffee and held the mug upside down. "All done." It was the pre-arranged signal for them to talk.

Aidan was beside her on the love seat in a flash. He took the mug from her and placed it on the table, never taking his eyes off hers.

Maddie warmed from his intense gaze. She was sure a blush that wasn't makeup colored her cheeks. She didn't need to look at her reflection in a mirror to know her eyes had regained their sparkle. All she needed was Aidan. His presence and his touch cured her of malaise, brought her appetite back. He made her come alive again.

"Black and short," Aidan observed, his fingers touching the ends of her hair on top of her shoulder. She'd taken it down from its ponytail earlier, to ease her headache.

"The clichéd breakup haircut," Maddie said in a self-mocking tone. It had been highlighted and midway down her back at the end of March. Her new hairstyle was supposed to have made her look more Filipina. Instead, it contrasted starkly with her eyes and skin, making them seem paler. By denying it, her Frenchness had become even more apparent. Still, she'd kept the shade because she was lazy and didn't have much interest in her appearance. "It's as black as I thought your and my father's hearts were when I had it cut."

Aidan sank to his knees before her, clasped both of her hands between his, and kissed them. "I'm sorry, Maddie. I could have fought harder not to involve you, but I didn't have the power to countermand orders made by three governments."

Maddie's chest contracted at the show of humility by such a proud man. She brought their joined hands to her cheek. "Please sit beside me, Aidan. I'm not going to talk down to you."

The look of gratitude he flashed her as he returned to his seat told her his level of comfort in lowering himself: zero. Being a supplicant didn't suit him. Aidan was born to command, not bend the knee. That he did it for her made her love him more.

Maddie kept her hands in his grasp. The warmth of his enveloping palms reassured her. "Hindsight is a gift I've only begun to appreciate these past couple of months. Of course you couldn't have told me about the mission. Even if you'd gone against orders, you wouldn't have been able to stop me from meeting my father. You'd have thrown away your career for nothing."

Aidan bared his teeth when she mentioned her father. His hands squeezed, almost reflexively. "I could have insisted I go with you from the start. He wouldn't have been able to talk to you like that if I was there."

She pulled out one hand to stroke Aidan's unshaven face, to get him to relax his clenched jaw. "Then you wouldn't have been able to catch him. He'd have continued to exchange information against your country for money. I wouldn't know the truth." It had hurt, but she'd accepted the fact.

She didn't anticipate closing the wound her father had dealt her anytime soon. Maybe in time, if he explained, she would forgive, but they would never have the relationship they once had. It saddened her. *C'est la vie.*

"Things were meant to happen as they did, Aidan. What he said to me that night, what he had been doing for the past twelve years were all on him, not on you."

"You were living with me, under my protection. I didn't protect you when you needed me most." His voice was tinged with regret.

Maddie hated seeing him so down on himself. She moved to sit on his lap, to give him, and herself, comfort. "You did as much as you possibly could. Before he let me go, the other American told me you'd provided the information that cleared me of all charges. But I wasn't ready to hear it then. I was too raw. It was pain I'd never experienced before. I hadn't developed an immunity. That's why it took me nine weeks to let you know I'm ready."

He didn't speak for a while; he just kept stroking her arms and hair compulsively. "What changed?"

Maddie's lips twitched. "Let's just say I was visited by an angel." Her friend's arrival had been timely. Angela had given her the push she'd needed to take the step towards reconciling with Aidan. "Angels, actually," she corrected, thinking of Hui Min and Noir.

"Whoever they were, I'm grateful. If you hadn't shown up today, I was planning to fire Vikram and deliver the food myself."

She reared back to frown at him. "Don't you dare fire Vik and his Bollywood eyes. I will leave you again."

Aidan laughed at the joke and pulled her close to his chest again. "I'm kidding. He's been my only connection to you for the past two months. I'll hire him permanently, even if I have to invent a job."

"Thank you. I can think of something at work too. If it wasn't for him, for the meals you sent, I'd have starved during the weekends. There was no—*oof*!"

Maddie found herself flat on her back, Aidan covering her mouth with his own, his tongue seeking and tangling with hers, filling her with the taste she'd missed so much. It was uniquely Aidan—sweet, dark, and utterly delicious. She joyously returned the kiss, pouring all her pent-up desire into the meeting of lips. To her astonishment, just as quickly as he swooped in, he withdrew, leaving her wanting more.

"Open your eyes, Maddie."

She hadn't realized she'd closed them. When she obeyed Aidan's command, it was to see his eyes, staring at her: bright blue and so hot, she felt seared by them.

"I'm sorry for falling on you like a hungry beast. I've been starved for you. I didn't think to check if you're physically able to match my wants." He raised her to sit between his legs, and he enfolded her in a hug so loose, his arms didn't touch her back. "I'm scared even doing this; I don't want to hurt you more than I already have."

Maddie returned his embrace. Hers was tight, although her arms couldn't reach all the way around him. "You won't. You can't. I'm stronger than I look. The only way you can hurt me is if you tell me you don't love me." He'd never said it. In actions, he'd told her in hundreds of different ways. She wanted the words.

He pulled back a few inches, cupped her face, and gazed into her eyes. "I love you, Maddie-mine. I have for a long time. That's why I wanted you to live with me. I didn't recognize the feeling for what it was until you left me."

Heart bursting with joy, Maddie brushed a kiss on his lips. More words needed to be said. "I love you too, Aidan. I wouldn't have accepted your offer of a Singapore fling if I hadn't been more than halfway in love with you already. You're the only one who has the power to break my heart and put it back together again, as you just did."

He dropped his forehead to hers and said against her lips, "I'm sorry I offered you less than what you deserve. I am sorry I gave our relationship an expiration date."

She stroked his jaw; the bristles tickled her palm. "Don't be. I wanted you however I could get you. It never occurred to me to ask for more. I thought being together was enough. Until it wasn't." She shook off the negative thought. It was over. "Our fling ended nine weeks ago, Aidan. We'll start afresh today."

"There shall be no end date. This is not a fling, Maddie-mine, but a commitment." His voice was gruff, weighted by the seriousness of his promises.

"A commitment. I love the sound of that." Maddie smiled against his lips. Attached to the word was an inherent promise that appealed to her, even though she'd vowed to live in the here and now. Their future would take care of itself if they made the most of today. "You know what I'd love even better?" She swung her legs down and pushed herself to her feet. "If we sealed that commitment in our bed." She held out her hands to Aidan, tugged him to stand. "Make love with me, Aidan. I've missed you. I missed us together."

In response, he picked her up and with long strides, took her to their bedroom. With infinite care, he laid her on the bed. Despite his gentleness, she couldn't help but wince. Her shirt had bunched beneath her, causing it to rub against her sore back.

"What happened? Did I hurt you?" Aidan sprang off the bed, worry etched on his face.

Maddie sat up. "No. It's my new tattoo. Angela bandaged it before she left yesterday afternoon to protect it from the filthy river water, but I might have loosened the bandage with all my activities this morning." She took off her shirt and bra. Half-naked, she lay back down, this time on her stomach, and looked at Aidan over her left shoulder. "Can you please remove the bandage so my skin can breathe?"

Aidan sat beside her, the expression on his handsome face concerned. "I thought your back felt weird when I carried you. I figured it was an undershirt or something."

Maddie watched him as he carefully peeled off the long gauze from the middle of her back, revealing one letter at a time.

"*Carpe diem*," he read out loud. His fingers traced the outer edges of each word, scratching at the leftover adhesive. He stretched out beside her, his hand continuing to caress, to build the fire. "When did you get it done? And why?"

Maddie shivered in delight. His touch provided both relief from the itch and the slow-burning heat. "Last Sunday, after my first time at paddling, I decided to get a tattoo. For me, this describes my attitude towards the future after I returned to you." She turned to face him. "I don't know if tomorrow will come, and if it does, what will happen. I only know I want to spend my todays with you from now on."

Aidan scooted closer, placed an arm around her, and kissed her lightly. "I want that too. I want to be beside you in the present and in the future. I love you, Maddie-mine."

Maddie kissed him right back. "And, I love you, Aidan-mine." She pushed him to his back and clambered on top. Grinning, she reached for the waistband of his shorts to pull them down. "Let's *carpe* the *diem* out of making love, shall we?"

He threw his shirt off and smiled back. "We shall."

EPILOGUE

Yam Seng [yum seng], exclamation – In Cantonese: "Cheers!" Usually heard at Chinese weddings.

"A captivating display like no other," Aidan recited, looking in admiration at his girlfriend. Her back to him, Maddie's jet-black hair styled in an elegant updo shone with a thousand little stars from the lights illuminating the hotel behind them. Sleek dress in traffic-stopping red lovingly caressed her returned curves. A long string of cultured pearls from her home country worn backwards around her throat aligned with the now completely healed "*Carpe Diem*" spine tattoo.

Spectra, the light and music show on the bay that would culminate the embassy's advanced Fourth of July celebration might be captivating. Madeleine Duvall, French Filipina public relations and events management expert, *his* woman, was absolutely dazzling. No question about it.

Stepping behind her, Aidan splayed his hand across Maddie's bare back above the dip in her garment and dropped a kiss on her shoulder to the right of the narrow strap, a breath away from her neck. She gave a slight shiver and sighed his name. Instant recognition: they both had that with each other.

Before straightening to his full height, he inhaled deeply of her glorious scent, the vanilla perfume he'd had Vikram's mother create in her shop in Little India. The hardworking kid continued to be part of their lives and was handsomely rewarded for his regular food deliveries to Maddie's East Coast apartment where they now spent their weekends. Maddie had thought about letting it go but decided to keep it for their many friends who wanted to visit this small but fascinating country.

Maddie let out another sigh, this one filled with sorrow. Aidan followed her gaze to the other side of the bay, to where the Merlion stood. Beyond that, the hotel where she'd last seen her father.

"You're thinking of him." He moved closer, careful to keep the medals and aiguillettes that decorated his mess dress from scratching her flawless skin.

"*Mon étoile, j'espère que tu pourrais me pardonner un jour.*" She repeated the lines from the note Jean-Marc had sent through the French ambassador.

My star, I hope you can forgive me one day. "Have you?" he asked, squeezing her shoulder in sympathy. Save for their reunion, they hadn't spoken the disgraced diplomat's name in a conversation this past month.

Maddie turned her head to meet his eyes. With her skyscraper heels, they were nearly the same height. "Yes. Maybe someday I can tell him in person."

Aidan pressed closer in response. He kept quiet to avoid the urge to reveal what he knew. Someday could be sooner than Maddie expected. Jean-Marc had been cooperating with US Intelligence and had named other diplomatic spies selling top secret information. It frustrated him that he couldn't tell her. He kept his fingers crossed that the payoff of a future meeting between father and daughter would be enough to justify his lie of omission. After all, he'd been the one who had requested the letter from father to daughter.

They'd vowed that honesty be a cornerstone of their relationship. So were trust, respect, and love. His work was a gray area they'd agreed to take on a case-to-case basis. This case held the possibility of being one of those "easier to ask for forgiveness than to ask for permission" kind of deals.

Aidan glanced at Maddie's profile, serene now after a short bout of melancholy. They'd been happy this past month. She'd gained back the weight and color she'd lost when they broke up, and they had taken up dragon boat racing as their regular Sunday fun day activity.

He wanted to remind her of the good days, not the bad one in the past. Striving for a light tone, he remarked, "Families, huh. Can't choose them, can't get rid of them forever."

It gratified him to see her lips curve. "Ha! You love your family. I'm looking forward to meeting them all in December."

At his brother and her best friend's wedding—their initial reason for starting this relationship. Tracing the letters of her new tattoo, Aidan found himself giving words to an impulsive thought. "What do you think about being introduced to them earlier than that?"

She turned to face him, her brows knotted in confusion. "I already know Craig is coming in two weeks."

He reached for her hands and laced their fingers. This felt right. "I mean go with me to New York. Meet Ma and Da and Darcy."

If the show was anything like the pleasure that lit up her face, it would be a spectacular one. "I'd love to. When?"

"How about the week of Singapore National Day in mid-August? We'll be here for two more years; we can participate in the celebrations some other time. I can't wait any longer for my family to get to know you."

She pressed a sweet kiss on his lips. "I can't either. Thank you for sharing your family with me."

Had they been anywhere else than a public space in Singapore, Aidan would have prolonged the kiss. But he was in his formal military uniform, representing his country, so he turned Maddie around and satisfied himself with a mere embrace.

Maddie understood the significance of meeting his family. If she didn't, she would soon. Blake had had his moment last year. Now it was his turn to introduce the woman he loved to his family. He knew Ma had another ring saved for him to give to his future wife. It was time to collect it.

Cheers went up as the colors of the rainbow lit up the night sky of Singapore, along with the soaring fountains that danced in time with instrumental music, fulfilling their promise to captivate. Aidan was enchanted, all right. Not by the show, but by the woman in his arms.

Looking around at the crowd, at pairs like him and Maddie, at Kalvin and Hui Min, Nate and Noir,

Aidan couldn't help but think how lucky he and Blake had been to fall for women who were best friends.

He worried for Craig, who had gotten larger the longer he stayed in Koh Samui. As far as he could tell, his brother was still in mourning and hadn't gone out on a date yet. If he didn't want to replace his Thai girlfriend with a compatriot, maybe he would go out with a Filipina. Like Angela, Maddie's friend who was based in the same place.

Good things come in threes. Tomorrow, he and Maddie would call Blake and Krista to set Operation Samui in motion. Tonight, he and Maddie would celebrate America's birthday.

###

AUTHOR'S NOTE

I hope you enjoyed reading Maddie and Aidan's story as much as I enjoyed writing it. SINGAPORE FLING is the longest book I've ever done because this pair of lovers wanted their story told exactly as you've read it.

I want to reiterate that everything military-related in this book is unclassified information. It is easily verifiable online. SINGAPORE FLING is a work of fiction. If the characters and scenes resemble the reader's personal experience, I swear that's pure coincidence.

The Singlish translations are from various sources. Among them:
- http://www.singlishdictionary.com/
- www.singlish.net
-https://guidesify.com/blog/2017/08/13/singlish-phrases-define-singapore/

The characters use the measurement system from their country of origin. Thus, Maddie measures in meters, grams, and Celsius while Aidan thinks in terms of the US customary system–miles, pounds, and Fahrenheit. Singapore adapts the metric system.

If this is your introduction to my writing and you like what you've read, you may also want to check out BORACAY VOWS and NEW YORK ENGAGEMENT. They tell the story of Krista and Blake, the pair who started it all.

The next full-length novel in the CARPE DIEM CHRONICLES series is SAMUI HEAT, with Angela and Craig bonding over food and rock climbing. Watch out for it in Spring 2020.

For bonus content, check out my website www.maidamalby.com. You'll find photos of all the places and food I've mentioned in the series, as well as sneak peeks of my works-in-progress. If you have any questions or comments, you can contact me at maidamalby@gmail.com. You can also find me on Facebook (Maida Malby), Twitter (@MaidaMalby), and Instagram (@carpediemchronicles). And if you liked my book, please leave a review. I'd really appreciate it, and it'll help new readers find it. Thank you.

Made in the
USA
Columbia, SC